RICK HOLMAN
Takes a Shower

For maybe a couple of minutes I just stood there letting the hot water gently cascade all over me, and feeling my headache slowly disappear. Then something warm and soft pressed against the length of my back. Two hands appeared in front of me and began gently to soap my chest and stomach.

"You seemed to be tuckered out," a soft voice murmured in my ear. "I figured the least I could do was help."

The feminine hands strayed lower and lower until I felt a very definite physical reaction. "Ah!" the voice in back of me purred. "Not too tired."

We will send you a free catalog on request. Any titles not in your local book store can be purchased by mail. Send the price of the book plus 50¢ shipping charge to Belmont Tower Books, P.O. Box 270, Norwalk, Connecticut 06852.

Titles currently in print are available for industrial and sales promotion at reduced rates. Address inquiries to Tower Publications, Inc., Two Park Avenue, New York, New York 10016, Attention: Premium Sales Department.

CARTER BROWN

The Phantom Lady

BELMONT TOWER BOOKS • NEW YORK CITY

A BELMONT TOWER BOOK

Published by

Tower Publications, Inc.
Two Park Avenue
New York, N.Y. 10016
Published by arrangement with Alan G. Yates
Copyright © 1980 by Horowitz Publications

All rights reserved
Printed in the United States of America

Chapter 1

Her straight blonde hair was brushed sleekly against the sides of her head and just reached the nape of her neck. She was wearing a black silk shirt with the top four buttons undone to reveal the cleavage between her firm pointed breasts, and matching black pants. Way down there between her breasts a silver medallion nestled, hanging from a heavy chain of silver links. The expensive strapwatch buckled tight around her wrist and cradled in thick black leather. Her name was Sandy Parker and she was an agent who sold talent. Finally, the droning sound of her voice stopped and her polished blue eyes looked at me.

"Am I boring you, Rick?"

"Yes," I said. "Frankly."

"I'm sorry." Her voice was cold. "Maybe you need another drink?"

"Or maybe you'll break down and tell me why we're here," I suggested.

She thought about it for a few seconds then said, "We've got trouble, Rick."

"Like the Lone Ranger?"

"What?"

"It's an old story. The Lone Ranger told Tonto they'd got trouble because there were a thousand Sioux waiting for them in the pass and Tonto said, 'What do you mean, *we've* got trouble? *I'm* an Indian.'"

"Jesus!" she said, in a strangled voice.

"So tell me about your trouble."

"I used the collective 'we' meaning me, and one of my clients." She took a deep breath. "You pompous shit!"

"So who is your client?"

"She also happens to be my very good friend. It goes a lot deeper than just an agent-client relationship. I'm very concerned for her."

"But you can't remember her name."

"I'm talking about Alison Vaile."

The memory banks made a small clunking sound inside my head. An English actress originally, I remembered. They had brought her out to the old dying Hollywood in the mid-Sixties with a great fanfare of publicity trumpets. She was cast in the mold of Grace Kelly and Deborah Kerr, they had said. A genuine lady who was not only beautiful but could also act. Some carefully vague references were made to her appearances at the Old Vic and with the Royal Shakespeare Company. Her first movie had gotten her good reviews and had died at the box office, then three stinkers had followed in a row.

After a long interval came a couple of spaghetti westerns where she stood around, looking like an English rose, while the hero picked his nose in between blowing the intestines out of innocent bystanders with a double barreled shotgun. Then there had been an even longer interval followed by a Broadway play—an English import—which had run all of eight performances. And then, nothing.

"What's she been doing lately?" I asked politely.

"Almost nothing," Sandy said. "As you goddamned well know, Rick Holman. Nothing for the last two years, but now she's gotten the chance at a series of commercials for network television."

"Big deal!"

"It's worth a quarter-million dollars."

"Like I said," I repeated, in a hushed voice. "Big deal!"

"You know what it's like now," she went on. "What with people starting to sue the star of the commercial if they're dissatisfied with the product. Or if they figure the star has a bad image because there's something nasty lurking in their background, they'll sue and claim it's misrepresentation of the product. Before any sponsor is about to take the risk right now they want to be sure their star is squeaky-clean."

"You mean Alison isn't?"

"I don't know."

"But you have your suspicions."

Sandy shrugged tightly. "Something's bothering her and it has been from the moment this deal was first mentioned. Maybe you know she was married a couple of times? The first was over before she left England and when she made those dreadful Italian westerns, I think she temporarily went out of her mind. She married her co-star."

"Duane Larsen."

"You know what kind of an actor he is," she said bitterly. "Every time he openes his mouth, his horse steps into it. He believed in a marriage between two equal partners, he told her, and to prove it he'd get stinking drunk every second week and beat the hell out of her. The marriage dragged on for a couple of years and then she left him when she couldn't take any more and got a divorce."

She took time out to sip her drink. "The whole lousy marriage had shaken her up and just about destroyed any confidence she had left. And her career wasn't going anyplace, either. She's never talked about the time after she left him and still won't talk about it, either."

"That's where something nasty lurks in her background?"

"I figure it's likely. After the divorce Alison said she had to get away from everything and she did, for a whole year. Then, one morning about a year back, I found her sitting in my office waiting for me. She wanted to go back to work, she said, and maybe I could help her. I took her back to my apartment because she had no place else to go. It took her a long time to get back to normal, whatever the hell that is. But I finally figured she was ready. I got her a nice little cameo piece with Stellar in their new prestige blockbuster with a twenty million budget. Then came the offer for the commercials and, right off, she freaked. She's running scared, Rick, and I don't know why."

"You've asked her?"

"Obviously! She gives me a lot of junk about it being bad for her image, and I keep asking what image? So that doesn't get us very far. If she does the commercials it means she'll go network just after the movie's been released and it will be fantastic for her. But she just refuses to even talk about it. It's gotten so we're hardly even talking to each other anymore."

"You figure she won't do the commercials because she's frightened some skeleton will come leaping out of her past and destroy her," I said. "And that skeleton belongs to the year after she divorced Duane Larsen, and before she turned up at your office."

"Right." She nodded her head vigorously.

"There has to be more," I said.

"You're a suspicious bastard, Holman!"

"And right, too."

"And right, too," she said reluctantly. "She's been getting these calls from some man. She won't tell me who he is, or what he wants. But I listened on the extension a couple times. His name is Pete and he calls Alison 'Gloria.' At first I figured it was some kind of a tired gag, but now I think it's more than that. He kept on asking her to meet him and she kept on saying she was finished with all that. Then, when he called last night, he said if she wouldn't visit with him, he'd visit with her at the apartment. That did it up just fine! She's going to meet him tonight at seven-thirty in a bar."

"This bar?"

"This bar."

"What else does this Pete say?"

"Nothing much. Keeps on talking about all the good times they had, and she keeps telling him they weren't good times. Gloria! What the hell kind of a name is that?"

"What did she tell you about the calls?"

"She said it was a friend of Duane Larsen's, a creep she'd prefer to forget. Alison is a lousy liar."

"What does she look like now?"

"About the same as she always did. She's a little older but it doesn't show. Still with the long blonde hair and she's put on a little weight, but it's in the right places."

"Okay," I said. "I'll stick around until they show." I checked my wristwatch and saw it was a quarter of seven. "How about you?"

"I'm going back to the office to catch up on a couple of contracts," she said. "What really hurts is she's too scared to confide in me."

"Has she got any money?"

"Only what she got paid for the cameo piece," Sandy said. "They knew they could buy her cheap and they did."

"Did she have any money when she turned up at your office that morning?"

"About all she had was the clothes she was wearing," Sandy said, in a neutral voice.

"So whatever it is Pete wants, it's not money," I said. "Maybe a piece of the commercials? You did say a quarter-million dollars?"

"Maybe." She didn't sound impressed. "I have a hunch it's got nothing to do with money. It's not love, either. She's so goddamned scared of him she can hardly speak whenever he calls."

"Maybe I should talk with Duane Larsen," I said. "Where will I find him?"

"He lives on Benedict Canyon." Her polished blue

eyes looked at me suspiciously. "What are you going to tell him? About Alison, I mean."

"That her agent is worried about her," I said. "Larsen will understand. He knows agents have ten percent of your life. I don't have to tell him how it is with the other ninety percent."

"I guess that sounds okay," she said, in a grudging voice. "I don't want you spreading this all over town, Holman."

"Rick Discretion Holman is my name," I told her.

"I should go," she said. "In case Alison decides to be real early for her date. You'll let me know what happens?"

"If anything," I promised.

She thought about it for a few seconds then said, "Do you want any money, or anything?"

"Not until I've done something for it."

She picked up her pocketbook from the table and got onto her feet. I watched her walk out of the bar, the rounded cheeks of her bottom bouncing tautly under the tight black pants. Sandy Parker was a real attractive woman, but I couldn't help wondering what kind of a relationship she had with Alison Vaile, exactly.

I ordered a fresh drink from the waiter and decided to string it out over the next half-hour, or until Alison Vaile finally showed. Five slow minutes crept past and then this little guy almost crept into the bar with a statuesque redhead on his arm. She must have been close to six feet tall in her high heels, and was wearing a white sweatshirt and lemon-colored tightfit pants. On the front of the sweatshirt was a vividly colored transfer of a fighting cockerel and underneath was the caption: BIONIC COCK. It seemed to be self-explanatory. Her full breasts jutted proudly and bounced with each step she took. The tight-fit pants showed off her generously-rounded hips and long legs to definite advantage. The little guy guided her swiftly to the banquette next to mine and was about to sit down when I said, "Hi, there, Manny!"

He frozed in a crouched position while his magnified eyes revolved desperately in back of the thick lenses.

"What's the matter, Mr. Kruger?" the redhead asked, in a wondering voice. "You get something caught in your zipper?"

"This is a time when I want to be private," Manny said bitterly, "and what do I get but Rick Holman!"

"You can be private, Manny," I told him. "I'll just sit here real quiet and listen to every word."

He straightened up again, grabbed hold of the girl's arm and guided her toward my banquette. I gave her a big smile as she sat down beside me and introduced myself.

"Hi." She gave me a slow sultry smile in return. "I'm Liz Moody."

"Who happens to be my new secretary," Manny said. "We've had an exhausting day at the studios and I thought the least I could do was buy her a drink."

"Mr. Kruger is a real sweet boss," Liz confided, in a breathless whisper.

Stellar is the last of the studio giants and Manny is their publicity director. He also goes through secretaries faster than DeMille used to go through epics. They last maybe a couple of months and then they move on. It has something to do with Manny's manic-depressive personality, I've always figured.

"Why are you spying on me, Rick?" he asked, right on cue.

"*You're* spying on *me*," I said. "Who followed me into this bar?"

He was still trying to figure that one out when the waiter arrived at the table.

"I'll have a Harvey Ballbanger," Liz Moody told him.

"*Wall* banger," Manny corrected her.

"Well, I guess I wouldn't know for sure." She giggled suddenly. "I mean, me being a girl, and all."

Manny winced, then told the waiter he'd have the same.

"Are you in the movies, Rick?" the redhead asked.

"He's a sordid peeper, is all," Manny said.

"A private detective?" Her eyes widened. "Gee! Do you have your own series and all?"

She had to be putting me on, I figured. Manny was concentrating real hard on me and I guessed he was trying to will me into dropping dead.

"What do you hear about Duane Larsen these days?" I asked idly.

"What should I hear about Duane Larsen?" he asked, in a suspicious voice.

"I guess it's just a rumor," I said.

"What rumor?"

The bigger the lie, the more likely Manny was to believe it, I remembered.

"I hear Stellar is about to sign him up for a remake of 'The Hunchback of Notre Dame.' He's playing the old Laughton part," I said.

"But he can't act!" Manny's face twitched convulsively. "Even in all those television oaters he can't act!"

"Like I said." I shrugged. "It's probably just a rumor."

"Nobody at the studio tells me anything anymore," he muttered. "Maybe there're ashamed to tell me. They should be ashamed! Duane Larsen playing the hunchback of Notre Dame? He probably figures it's a story about some football player!"

Right then Alison Vaile came into the bar. She stopped just long enough to check out the occupants, then walked across to an empty banquette on the other side of the room. So maybe she was a little older but she still looked great. The shoulder-length blonde hair was sleek and glittered with highlights. If the face was a little more plump, the high cheekbones still dominated. She was wearing a beautifully cut little black dress that discreetly accentuated all her abundant curves and they still looked just as firm as ever as she moved lithely across the room. Manny had turned his head to see what I was staring at and was visibly moved.

"Hey!" he said, in an awed voice. "There's Alison Vaile."

"Alison, who?" I said vaguely.

"Alison Vaile. She just finished a cameo role for us in a five-star epic."

I took another look and saw the guy heading toward her banquette. He was around forty and big for his age. The thatch of red hair had receded to about halfway back across his head and the naked white skin was heavily freckled. The thick drooping mustache made him look like a retired gunfighter. His crumpled suit didn't do anything for him, either. A fat cigar was clutched between two fingers of his right hand, and he was visibly sweating. At around thirty pounds overweight I figured he would sweat a lot, but there were still some powerful muscles attached to his big frame.

"Maybe I should go over there and say hello?" Manny worried about it for a couple of seconds. "I mean, I am Stellar's publicity director and it's up to me to show the flag, right?"

"Gee!" the redhead sounded impressed. "I never knew the studio has its very own flag."

Manny got up onto his feet, squared his thin shoulders, then marched across the room.

"Your hair is the wrong color for it," I told the redhead.

"For what?"

"It should be blonde," I said, "it's traditional. Nobody ever believes redheads are dumb."

"Mr. Kruger fired his last secretary because he figured she was too smart," Liz Moody confided. "So I'll play it any way he wants. It beats the hell out of sitting around the typing pool all day."

"You can come and lie around my place all night if you want," I said generously. "It'll make an interesting change for you."

"Oh, wow!" she said frostily.

"Real stupid of me," I apologized. "I should have remembered you're probably happy to stay home nights with just your bionic cock to keep you company."

Her face froze for a moment, then she gurgled with laughter.

Then Manny was back with his face a bright red color. He dropped down into his seat and took a swift gulp of his drink.

"The bum with her told me to get lost," he said, in

a choked voice. "Me, the publicity director of Stellar Studios!"

"I can't believe that," I said, in a shocked voice, and the redhead made faint whimpering sounds.

"I walked up and said a polite hello to Miss Vaile," Manny continued in a shaky voice, "and before she could answer this bum tells me her name is Gloria LaVerne, and she wouldn't get my rocks off for me if I owned the goddamned studios. Then he tells me if I don't get lost he'll tear off my arms and stuff them down my throat!"

"So maybe it is Gloria LaVerne, whoever she is?" I suggested.

"That's Alison Vaile," Manny snarled. "And what the hell is she doing with a bum like him?"

"You really want to know?" I asked.

"Would I ask out loud if I didn't?" he demanded.

I got up and walked across to where the blonde lady and the retired gunfighter were sitting. Alison Vaile looked up at me, then clear through me, as only a genuine lady can. I gave the guy a warm friendly smile.

"What the hell do you want?" he asked, in a hoarse voice.

"It's for my friend, the midget." I pointed in Manny's direction. "He wants to know what a beautiful lady like Miss Vaile is doing in the company of a bum like you."

"He what?"

"He'd also like you to have a drink with him," I said.

I picked up his glass from the tabletop and carefully poured the contents down the front of his crumpled suit.

He pushed the table back and started to get up onto his feet. I carefully waited until he was about halfway, still in a crouching position and completely defenceless. Then I hit him straight between the eyes, putting all my weight in back of the punch. He fell back onto the banquette, his eyes vacant, then his head rolled slackly to one side. Alison Vaile made a small stricken sound deep in her throat and looked at me fearfully.

"Sorry about that, Miss LaVerne," I said politely. "It is Gloria LaVerne, right? I seem to remember you from someplace."

The color vanished from her face then she rose to her feet and walked quickly toward the door. A couple of waiters were approaching the table real fast and, out of the corner of my eye, I saw Manny and Liz Moody were bravely preparing to flee the bar. By the time the waiters reached me I had my wallet in my hand.

"He shouldn't have called me what he called me," I said, as I pulled a couple of twenties out of my wallet and put them flat on the table. "I guess this will take care of everything, right?"

"Sure," the nearest waiter said, the moment after my twenties vanished from the tabletop. "But you are leaving right now?"

I took a card out of my wallet and carefully tucked it into the limp gunfighter's pocket.

"Just in case he wants to sue, or something," I explained, then started walking toward the door.

Chapter 2

There was nobody waiting for me on the sidewalk and I wasn't exactly surprised. I picked up my car from the lot two blocks down from the bar and drove leisurely up to Benedict Canyon. A private road ran off at an acute angle and was protected by a steel mesh barrier and a guard post. A classic example of the very rich exercising their democratic rights. A couple of uniformed private cops were on duty inside the guardhouse. They watched while I stopped the car in front of the barrier and got out. Finally, one of them deigned to leave the guardhouse and find out what the hell it was I wanted.

"Private road," he said curtly. "You got to be known, or have a pass."

"I want to visit with Duane Larsen," I told him.

"You don't visit with nobody without a pass."

"Maybe you could call him for me," I said. "My

name's Rick Holman. Tell him it's about his ex-wife, Alison Vaile."

"You got to be kidding!"

"Twenty bucks?"

"Mr. Larsen might not like to be disturbed right now," he said.

"Thirty?"

"You mention fifty, I could stick my neck out."

"Fifty," I said. "I just thought I'd mention it."

"Okay."

He came right up to the mesh fence and held out his hand. I gave him the money then watched him walk back to the guardhouse and pick up the phone. His partner watched me carefully the whole time in case, I guessed, I was some kind of an urban guerilla with a couple of grenades in my hip pocket. The sun was starting to slide down over the horizon and the sky above the smog line was beautifully clear. Somewhere inside the compound a couple of dogs barked savagely; either Dobermans or German Shepherds, for sure. Who wanted to be this rich, I wondered? The guard reappeared and came back to the fence.

"He'll see you." He sounded almost disappointed. "The fifth house down. Don't stop on the way."

I got back into the car and started the motor. The guard waved to his partner and the mesh barrier lifted. I drove on down the private road, counting off the houses until I reached the fifth. The house was a big split-level, with a view of the valley beneath. There was a four-car garage and a swimming pool with a lanai beside it. As I parked the car the floodlights above the pool came on in a kind of illuminated welcome. Then the front door opened and a guy walked out onto the porch. I got out of the car and walked to meet him.

Duane Larsen had to be in his early forties but the thick coarse blond hair showed no sign of thinning. The amiable-ugly face was his trademark; the broken nose, the deep scar on his left cheek, and the bleak stare from the cold blue eyes, were all part of an invaluable trademark. Whenever Duane Larsen rode the owlhoot trail you started feeling sorry for the owlhoots. Boy! Were they going to get theirs! He was around six foot tall but looked shorter because of the width of his shoulders and the huge barrel chest. The belly was sagging a little over the clasp of his belt, I noticed, but the swagger was just as good as ever.

"You're Holman." His voice was a deep growl.

"Hi."

His right hand enveloped mine and he tried real hard to wring the feeling out of my fingers, but it's all in the grip.

"Come on into the house," he said.

I followed him inside the house, into the spacious living room where everything looked sparkling fresh like it had just moved in from the color pages of *Good Housekeeping*. The only thing out of character was the girl with one elbow leaning on the bar.

She was tall with long straight black hair that fell down across her shoulders. Her dark brown eyes had a limpid look and her wide mouth a strong protruding lower lip. She was wearing high-heeled sandals and white lace bikini briefs. Her breasts were full and deep, the coral-colored nipples large and semi-tumescent. The skimpy briefs were pulled tight over the swell of her mound and indented her slit.

"You want a drink?" Larsen asked.

"Bourbon on the rocks, thanks," I said.

The girl made the drink then brought it across to where I was standing, her breasts jiggling with each step. I thanked her as I took the glass out of her hand and she gave me a small smile in return.

"Man's talk," Larsen said. "You want to get lost for a while, Julie."

"Sure," she said, in a demure voice.

I watched the taut bounce of her bottom under the tight briefs as she walked out of the room. Larsen gave me a knowing grin.

"Known as a Larsen specialty," he said. "I always keep at least one around the house the whole time. You never know when you might get a sudden urge."

"It goes with the image," I agreed.

He frowned. "Don't give me any of that shit, Holman. I do what I want when I want, and everybody else can get screwed."

"You're not drinking?" I asked him.

"I'm on the wagon right now," he said shortly. "You want to talk about my ex-wife, the frigid bitch?"

"That's right."

"I know about you, Holman. Your reputation, anyway. So what's sweet little Alison been doing that she shouldn't?"

"Her agent's worried about her," I said. "Sandy Parker."

"That dyke," he sneered.

I told him the story about the television commercials worth a quarter-million dollars and how Alison

Vaile was refusing to do them. He knew about the pressures now on actors doing commercials so he got the point fast.

"There's a long gap after the divorce before she went to Sandy Parker, like a year," I said. "I'm hoping you can tell me something about that year like what she did, where she went, like that?"

"It figures she'd wind up with a dyke," he said. "The sex was lousy with her from the very beginning. For a while there I figured it had to be me." He took a deep breath and puffed out his barrel chest. "Me! One of the biggest bulls in the business. It got so bad I'd get real drunk and start hitting her." He looked at me soberly. "Can you imagine that, Holman? Duane Larsen, hitting a woman!"

"It's real hard," I said solemnly.

"So we finally got a divorce," he said. "I figured she had me hogtied right here in California with the community settlement laws, and all. But said she wasn't interested in property, all she wanted was money. So I gave her some."

"How much?"

"Seventy-five grand," he said casually. "I figured it was cheap at the price."

"When she showed up at Sandy Parker's office a year later she didn't have a dime."

"Is that right?" He thought about it for a couple of seconds then raised his voice. "Julie!"

She sauntered back into the room and looked at him. "What?"

"I'll have a martini," he said.

"You know what the doctor said."

"Screw the doctor!"

She grinned. "Not at his prices!"

Julie walked across to the bar and set up a shaker. I sipped my own drink delicately and waited for Larsen to say something.

"Maybe that's what she told Sandy Parker," he said. "It didn't have to be true."

"You have any idea where she went after she left you?"

"Her career was shot," he said. "That Broadway play that folded was the tag-end. But she had my seventy-five grand when she threw her bags into the car and drove away so I wasn't bleeding for her. I didn't ask where she was going, I was just goddamned glad to see her go."

"But you don't know where she went."

"You want it in a glass?" Julie asked.

"Just give me the shaker," Larsen told her.

She brought it across to him, her full breasts jiggling with every step. He grabbed the shaker out of her hand and tilted it to his lips. The apple in his throat jumped convulsively three or four times before he finally lowered the shaker.

"That's just right," he said.

"I think I'll go take a swim," Julie said. "All that breast-stroke is supposed to keep them nice and firm." She turned toward me slightly. "What do you think, Mr. Holman?"

"I think they're nice and firm," I said.

"Get out of here, you two-bit whore," Larsen told her, without any rancor in his voice. "We're still talking man's talk."

"I figured I was, too," she said.

"No," Larsen said, after Julie had left the room. "I don't know where she went but I could make a couple of guesses. Why don't we sit down."

He sprawled on the couch and I sat in an armchair facing him. Another gigantic gulp from the shaker made him burp slightly.

"First drink in a whole week," he said. "It makes for a lousy world when you see it sober."

"A couple of guesses," I reminded him.

"She was a lady," he said. "A real English out-of-the-top-drawer lady, and I'd been playing gunslingers in Westerns all my life. That was her big attraction for me and it was all phoney. She was no more a lady than I'm a fag! I figured she'd enjoy the social bit but I was wrong about that, too. During the whole time we were together she only ever made three friends at most. Eddie Braun was one. He used to be a friend of mine until I suspected he was screwing Alison on the side. Maye he was, and maybe he wasn't. But we don't see each other anymore."

"Eddie Braun?" I queried.

"You don't know Eddie?" He sounded genuinely surprised. "The best pimp in the business. He's supposed to be in the personal public relations racket but Eddie can always find you the best-looking and most athletic girls in all California. He's got an office on the Strip. 'Media On,' is the crappy name of his outfit."

"What about the other friends she made?"

He took time out to lower the constantly-shrinking level of the martini shaker another couple of inches.

"Sylvia was the fifth wife of the late Benjamin Madden," he said. "Bennie married them when they were young and beautiful and divorced them a few years later. But he never made the mistake of marrying them in California. More like Nevada with a marriage contract signed before the event. He inherited the Madden retail store complex and never did a day's work in all his life. He meet Sylvia in Europe and was so excited about her he forgot all about the contract. Two months after they were married he dropped dead of a coronary. She inherited everything. I guess she and Alison got along fine because they were a couple of fake ladies together."

"Where would I find Sylvia Madden?"

He yawned, and scratched his chest under his shirt. "She's got a house in the Palisades, but then she's got an apartment in New York, never mind the one in London and the one in Paris." His eyes opened wide for a moment. "You're not going to quote me to her friends, Holman?"

"I wouldn't dream of it," I said. "There was one more, you said?"

"Charles Stratton," he said. "English, like her. Sounds like he's talking into a tumbler the whole goddamned time. I don't think he was screwing her on the side because I figure he'd think screwing was vulgar. Got a look on his face like somebody just shoved a slice of lemon up his left nostril the whole time. He lives in Bel Air and I guess he has to do something but he never talked about it."

"Anybody else?"

"That's them," he said. "You want another drink, help yourself, Holman."

"I'm doing fine, thanks."

He finished what was left in the shaker and dropped it to the floor.

"You ever met a Gloria LaVerne?" I asked him.

"You've got to be kidding. Nobody is called Gloria LaVerne!"

His eyelids slowly drooped shut and I guessed he was in for an early night. I finished my drink, returned the empty glass to the bartop, then walked out into the kitchen. The darkhaired girl was drinking coffee.

"Let me guess," she said. "He finished the shaker and passed out cold, right?"

"Right," I agreed. "Are you one of Eddie's girls?"

"Sure, I'm one of Eddie's rentagirls," she said. "Duane rents one of us for a week at a time. It's almost like a rest cure when he's drinking. He's been off it for the last three days and last night he almost made it."

"He has a drinking problem?"

"A real big one the doctor told him, but it doesn't seem to worry Duane too much."

"You know a girl called Gloria LaVerne?"

"Not that I remember."

"What kind of a guy is Eddie?"

"A bastard," she said. "But you can make a good living being one of his rentagirls and you get to meet some real interesting people here and there."

"I guess Duane has to be the exception."

She grinned. "You could be right about that. I was listening to the both of you just now. It's one of the advantages of an open-plan house like this. The sound carries all over."

"So?"

Her dark eyes were serious and her nipples were hard and pointed. Maybe it was the night air filtering through the open window?

"It's none of my business," she said. "But you seem to be a nice guy. Some kind of a detective, I guess. If you come up against Eddie Braun, handle him gently or you could get hurt."

"Thanks for the advice," I said.

"Maybe I could help?" She thought about it for a couple of seconds. "I don't know anything about that Alison Vaile, except I could feel sorry for her being married to good ole Duane at one time. But about Eddie I know a lot."

"Thanks again," I said.

"Don't contact me through Eddie's office," she said quickly. "Maybe it would be better if I called you sometime when I'm free, okay?"

I took a card out of my wallet and gave it to her. She smiled vaguely then tucked the card into the waistband of her lacey briefs. It looked at home there, all nice and snug, and somehow it gave me a lonely feeling.

Chapter 3

I stopped off for a quick steak on my way home, so it was around ten-thirty when I arrived back at the house. The key opened the front door as usual. I stepped into the front hall and switched on the light as usual. Then something slammed down on the back of my head which was distinctly unusual. I went down on all fours and a boot connected painfully with my rump and sent me sprawling full-length. It seemed like the hall light was flashing on and off intermittently and I wasn't sure where the hell I was, exactly. Then a hand grabbed my collar and dragged me into the living room. The light came on and whoever it was threw me into a chair. My head still hurt like hell and my vision wasn't too good.

"It makes me feel a little better," a harsh voice said. "Not much, just a little."

I kept my eyes tight shut for a few more seconds

then opened them slowly. No more sudden flashes and the room stayed still. It was something; not much, but something. The big guy sitting in an armchair facing me had receding red hair and a thick droopy mustache. I recognized him right off with no trouble at all. He stripped the cellophane wrapper off a big cigar then lighted it carefully.

"So maybe this is the way you get your kicks?" he said.

"What the hell are you talking about?"

"Leaving me your calling card and all," he said. "You want me to beat up on you some more, I don't mind." He grinned, showing slightly yellow teeth. "But that sucker-punch sure fooled me. You packed a hell of a lot of weight in it, Holman. Most masochists only like to get hurt themselves."

"I'd like a drink," I told him.

"Who wouldn't?" He looked at me carefully. "I'll make them. You wouldn't try to do anything stupid, would you? I mean, next time I'll break your goddamned neck!"

He walked over to the bar and made the drinks. Then he brought one over to me, holding the glass in his left hand and watching me real carefully as I took it from him. I took a sip while he retrieved his own drink from the bartop and brought it back to the armchair again.

"All I wanted was someplace quiet where we could talk," I told him. "That's why I left my calling-card with you."

"You went to all that trouble just so we could talk?" He grinned again. "Why didn't you just ask?"

"You wouldn't have listened."

"I guess you're right. So talk."

"I'm interested," I said. "Like how does Alison Vaile suddenly become somebody called Gloria LaVerne."

"I don't know any Alison Vaile," he said. "The broad I was with is Gloria LaVerne. I called her Gloria because that's her goddamned name."

"Is that right, Pete?" I said.

"Pete?" he said softly.

"Alison Vaile can make a lot of money out of doing a series of television commercials," I said. "But suddenly she's scared of doing them. Maybe it's because you keep on calling her the whole time and don't use her right name?"

"That agent-bitch," he said. "Listening on an extension."

"She was married to Duane Larsen," I said. "After the divorce she dropped out of sight for a year. Maybe it was during that time she became Gloria LaVerne."

"Don't try and find out, Holman," he said. "Because if you do it'll kill her. Tell your agent-bitch friend just that."

"Come on," I said. "For Pete's sake!"

"You want me to work you over again just to prove it?"

"A couple of sucker punches makes us even, I guess," I said. "But there won't be any sucker punches the second time around."

"I can take you any way at all," he said confidently.

"But it won't resolve anything."

"You're scared!"

"Try me."

We glared at each other like a couple of less-than-bionic fighting cockerels for a few seconds, then he grinned slowly.

"You're right," he acknowledged. "It won't resolve anything. There's a lot of dirty mud, Holman. You start stirring it up and something real nasty is going to drift to the surface. You won't believe this but I'm trying to stop it happening."

"You're right," I said. "I don't believe it."

"Maybe there's another way to convince you. I'll think about it."

The doorbell rang and he stiffened for a moment. "You expecting somebody?"

"There's this concealed bellpush in back of my head in the couch," I told him. "When I lean my head back an alarm goes off down at Headquarters and they send out all the L.A.P.D. right away."

He grinned sourly. "Okay. I guess I'll leave the same way as I came in, by the back door. It's a real cheap lock, Holman. But I'll be in touch."

"I can hardly wait," I assured him.

He left his empty glass on the bartop on his way to the kitchen. The doorbell rang again, so I got up off the couch and headed toward the front hall. I switched on the porch light then opened the front door. The darkhaired girl gave me an uncertain smile. In back of her on the driveway stood a beat-up Volks. Her name was Julie, I remembered, and now she was dressed. A black orlon sweater molded her breasts and tight jeans hugged her hips.

"Hi," she said, in a small voice.

"It's what they call an unexpected pleasure," I said. "Come on in."

"I'm not disturbing you, or anything?"

"I had a guest who was unexpected and no pleasure at all," I said, "but he just left."

I closed the front door behind her and led the way into the living room. She ran one hand lazily through her long hair as her dark brown eyes carefully surveyed the room.

"One shaker full of martinis is enough even for Duane Larsen," she said. "He won't wake up until sometime around noon tomorrow and he'll look dreadful, too. I got bored all by myself."

"How about a drink?"

"Rye on the rocks, thanks."

I went out to the kitchen on the pretext of getting some ice cubes to make sure my departing guest had departed. The kitchen was empty so I figured he had. I filled the bucket with ice cubes and went back into the living room.

"I also figured if you wanted to talk about Eddie Braun, now could be a good time," Julie said.

She sat down on the couch after I had given her a drink and I sat facing her in an armchair.

"You know a guy called Pete who maybe works for Braun?" I asked her. "Big guy around forty with red hair and a matching mustache. Looks like the tip of his nose is on fire."

"Him, I would remember," she said, "But I don't."

"So what else does Eddie Braun do apart from running a rentagirl racket?"

"He's supposed to handle personal publicity for people," she said. "Maybe the same clients who rent girls from him, like Duane Larsen? He's right in the heart of the high rent neighborhood and his offices are real big. So I guess he has to be successful at whatever else he does as well as the rentagirls."

"How many girls work for him?"

"I wouldn't know." She shrugged. "A lot, I guess."

"You're a mine of information, Julie."

She grinned slowly. "Eddie keeps a tight rein on all his girls. I was thinking, if Duane's ex-wife was all that friendly with Eddie she could have gone to work for him after the divorce."

"According to Duane he gave seventy-five thousand dollars as a settlement. It doesn't figure she needed money that bad she'd go to work for Braun."

"Maybe she did it for kicks?" She drank some of her drink. "I'm not being much of a help, right?"

"But it's nice to sit here and look at you," I said.

"Who is this Gloria LaVerne, anyway?"

"Somebody who was supposed to be a close friend of Alison Vaile after the divorce," I lied glibly.

"I could ask some of the other girls if they ever heard of her. Find out if she's ever worked for Eddie."

"Thanks," I said. "So what's a nice girl like you doing in the rentagirl racket?"

"Making a good living," she said evenly. "Getting a full sex life. Sometimes you get to screw with the most interesting people."

"Are Eddie's clients all big names like Duane?"

"Not all big names but they're all loaded with money," she said.

"Everybody involved must keep a tight mouth," I said. "One unhappy girl could blow the whole deal."

"Nobody's about to," she said. "Eddie's a firm believer in discipline. The first thing he shows you after you've gone to work for him is some pictures of what happened to a girl who developed a big mouth. They're not pretty!"

"He has his own bunch of goons?"

"I wouldn't know about a bunch. There's one, Mike Olsen, who always seems to be around his office." She shivered suddenly. "One of the girls told me she had an argument with Eddie over a pay-off so he had Olsen take her into a back room. He hurt the hell out of her! But taking great care the whole time that none of it would show and spoil any of her assets. She had to spend the next four days in bed and there wasn't one bruise to show for it, even."

"Suppose you wanted to quit?"

"You can quit," Julie said. "Provided you can show Eddie good reason and you don't try and walk out on a job that's already booked. It makes it a hell of a lot easier if you can come up with another girl to take your place."

She finished her drink then took the empty glass with her across to the bar. Mike Olsen sounded like Pete, I thought, but he obviously wasn't Pete because Julie would have recognized him from my description. Thinking thoughts like that were a big help all over. Julie made herself a fresh drink then leaned her elbows on the bartop and looked at me.

"I never thought to ask," she said. "You're not married, or anything?"

"No."

"You're not gay?"

"No."

"Just talkative, right?"

"Just tired," I said. "I think I'll take a shower before I go to bed."

She stared at me open-mouthed, her eyes not believing it, as I stood up then put my empty glass down on the coffee table.

"I come all the way over here and this is all there is to it?" she snarled at me.

"Thanks for the chitchat, anyway," I told her.

I walked out of the living room and down the three stairs that led to the bedroom-bathroom complex. It wasn't that complex when you got right down to it; just two rooms, but at least they were spacious. I stripped off my clothes and left them on the bedroom floor, then walked into the bathroom and turned on the shower.

For maybe a couple of minutes I just stood there letting the hot water gently cascade all over me, then felt the headache slowly disappear. The smart thing to do then was turn on the cold faucet and let the needle-spray tone me up. The hell with that! Why would I want to tone up all the muscles I'd just relaxed? And what kind of reflex was it that had me reaching for the soap? Only when I looked down I saw both my arms were still at my sides. Shades of, "Psycho!" The third arm kept on going until the hand grabbed the soap and the next moment they all disappeared. So the soap-stealing maniac of Beverly Hills was on the loose again.

Something warm and soft, firm but yielding, pressed against the length of my back. Two hands appeared in front of me and the one holding the bar of soap began to gently soap my chest while the other massaged my stomach.

"You seem so tuckered-out," a soft voice murmured in my ear. "I figured the least I could do was help."

The hands reversed themselves so the one holding the soap was now busy soaping my stomach and making a real good job of it, too.

The lower hand strayed lower still and I felt a very definite physical reaction.

"Ah!" the voice in back of me purred. "Not too tired."

The hands went on about their soothing work until I had to be the cleanest, and by now the horniest, Holman there ever had been. Then the soap was replaced and the hands withdrawn. As I turned around to face her the cold needle-spray hit me with icy force. For a stunned few seconds I just stood there, then made a frantic leap out of the shower stall.

"Poor little itty-bitty thing," Julie said, as she looked down at me. "Has the nasty needle-spray made him all limp and uninterested?"

My bathmaid was dressed as all bathmaids should be dressed, just in their skins. I looked at her proud jutting breasts, the soft swell of her belly that melted into a triangular profusion of tight black curls, and limp became distinctly less limp.

"It's disgusting," I said severely.

"I thought it was twitching," she said.

"Here's me, so clean I squeak when I move," I said, "and there's you just standing here absolutely filthy!"

"Not absolutely filthy," she objected. "Maybe a little bit grubby. It's the smog, you know."

I reached back into the shower and twisted the faucet until the hot water started running again, then picked up the soap.

"Your turn," I told her.

She stepped under the shower, keeping her head tilted so her hair wouldn't get wet. I got into the stall behind her and started on my merry soaping way. When my hand reached the lower curve of her belly, she obligingly parted her legs. I soaped very carefully between them, then up into the deep valley between the two cheeks of her bottom. By the time I had finished by rinsing off the soap with nimble control of the needle-spray—holding her firmly as the ice-cold water hit her more intimate parts and ignoring her wild screams of protest—she was at least as squeaky-clean as me. Toweling each other dry was the kind of exercise that beats the hell out of jogging any day of the week. Then we went into the bedroom.

Julie turned to face me and her arms went around my neck. Her breasts flattened against my chest and the soft warmth of her, as our fur intermingled, brought me to an immediate erection. My hands cupped the rounded firmness of her bottom and pulled her even closer against me. Our tongues wrestled for what seemed a long time and then, suddenly, we were stretched out on the bed.

"There's something I just remembered," she whispered into my ear. "You don't need to hurry, Rick. The rest of the night is on Duane Larsen!"

Chapter 4

Julie made breakfast the next morning, wearing just her skimpy white briefs. It's the kind of outfit that distracts a man from his morning coffee, and brings back memories of the previous night. She disappeared while I was still blissfully remembering, then returned fully-dressed.

"It was lovely, Rick," she said. "I had many, many orgasms. It made a great change from having to fake them. Maybe you noticed my happy grunts? When you're faking, you have to moan and scream a lot just to convince the clunkhead he's giving you a great time."

"Say thank you to Duane Larsen for the both of us," I said.

She pulled a face. "It was only a joke, Rick. A funny. One of those things you say hah-hah to, right?"

"Hah-hah," I grunted.

"Did it puncture your precious little male ego?" she asked, in a baby lisp. "Was the little man upset he was only getting it for free because somebody else had already paid for my time?"

"You know something?" I grinned at her. "You are a genuine goldplated bitch!"

"I have to run," she said. "Be there in time to show loving smypathy when he wakes up with a horrible hangover. Are you going to visit with Eddie Braun?"

"I guess so."

"You will forget to mention my name?" Her face was suddenly anxious.

"Anything you say, Gertrude," I assured her.

"Thank you, Edgar."

She leaned down and quickly kissed me on the cheek. "I hope we can have another shower together again soon."

"And next time don't forget to wash behind my ears," I told her.

The house was bleaker after she left. I finished my coffee and thought about the rest of the day ahead with no enthusiasm at all, then the phone rang.

"Rick?" The voice was hoarse, muted, and conspiratorial. Who else but Manny Kruger?

"How's everything, Manny?"

"That redheaded bastard you clobbered in the bar last night," he said. "He doesn't know my name, right?"

"Right."

"Not that I was worried," he said quickly. "I could handle him anytime. Did you know I'm a karate blue belt?"

"Black belt," I said automatically.

"I got them all colors," he said. "I was going to stay and help you but my secretary was so scared I didn't want her fainting, or anything."

"Sure, Manny," I said.

"You are my good friend, Rick Holman," he said. "The guy who's always there to get me and the studio out of an embarrassing situation. We have no secrets from each other and we've got absolute trust in each other." He sighed emotionally. "It's nice!"

"What do you want?"

"I talk of friendship and you figure I want something?" he said indignantly.

"Right."

"This remake of 'The Hunchback of Notre Dame,' with Duane Larsen playing the old Laughton role," he said. "I've been putting my ear to the studio ground this morning and nobody knows anything!"

"So?" I prompted.

"So it's just a stupid rumor," he said.

"My lips are sealed."

There was a faint gibbering sound in my ear so I hung up on him. The phone rang again thirty seconds later.

"Where do I find Sylvia Madden?" I said, the moment I picked up the phone.

"Sylvia Madden?" Manny sounded hysterical. "Who cares about that conniving bitch? When my best friend betrays me by joining some stinking conspiracy to keep me from knowing what's going on inside my own studio! The Palisades is where you find her. I could give you her private number, even, but I won't!"

"For a private number I could unseal my lips," I said.

"Unseal them," he said eagerly, "and I'll have my secretary call you back with the number."

"I heard it from the horse's mouth," I said. "From Duane Larsen himself."

"Some bastard has set up the whole secret project here." I could almost hear Manny thinking. "Who is Larsen dealing with at the studio?"

"He wouldn't tell me."

"Somebody right here in the studio is shafting me!"

"So shaft them right back."

"How?"

"Make a direct approach to Larsen," I said. "Tell him you're right behind the project and you want to develop it with him. He'll probably pretend the whole deal comes as a real surprise to him but don't let it faze you. When he tells whoever it is back at the studio the guy will have to quietly fade out of the picture and pretend he never knew anything about it, right?"

"Rick, my old buddy!" His voice shook with emotion. "You just could have the beginnings of a great idea there."

"Think about it," I said, "and don't forget to have your secretary call me back with that number."

I hung up and waited. A couple of minutes later the phone rang.

"Don't you feel embarrassed when you realize where the sun is shining from this morning?" the recognizable voice of Liz Moody enquired.

"Only when I look over my shoulder into a mirror," I said.

"I have that number for you. It's one of the rare ones, Mr. Kruger says."

"Thanks," I said, and wrote down the number when she gave it to me.

"Do you always beat up on people in bars?" she asked.

"It was being rejected by a beautiful redhead that did it," I told her. "Made me go like berserk."

"All that energy," she said thoughtfully. "Wasted on hitting another man."

"I'll hit you if you want," I said.

"It wasn't what I had in mind, exactly, Mr. Holman. You don't mind me calling you Mr. Holman, Rick?"

"I don't mind, Miss Moody."

She chuckled and it had a kind of wanton sound to it, the moment before she hung up.

I dialed the number she had just given me and a deep voice answered after the fouth ring.

"Sylvia Madden?" I asked.

"Who the hell else were you expecting on an unlisted number?" she said coldly. "Your Aunt Agatha? And I do mean the one who balls all the team right after the basketball game in senior high."

"I'm Rick Holman," I said. "I'd like to talk with you about a friend of yours called Alison Vaile."

"Hold it," she said. "I'm beginning to remember. Manny Kruger told me one time if I was ever in trouble, Rick Holman was the man to handle it for me. I guess there aren't two Rick Holmans in L.A.?"

"I'm the only one I know," I said helpfully.

"Alison Vaile is no friend of mine," she said. "I knew her at one time."

"That's the time I'd like to talk about," I said.

"All right," she said. "Drop in around six tonight and we can have a drink. You know the address?"

I said I didn't and she gave it to me. I said thanks and good-bye and she hung up. Maybe it was better than talking to Manny, but only a little.

Around thirty minutes later I arrived at the offices of "Media On." The front office had blow-up pictures of some of their clients lining the walls. A couple I vaguely recognized but the rest were strangers. The black receptionist with the Afro hair-do gave me a flashing smile. She was wearing a white silk shirt-dress and it fit real snug across her high firm breasts.

"Can I help you, sir?"

"I'm Rick Holman," I said. "I'd like to see Mr. Braun."

"Do you have an appointment?"

"Not even a poodle."

"Can I ask what it's about?"

"Girls," I said. "I want to rent one."

Her smile collapsed suddenly. "Would you take a seat, Mr. Holman, and I'll find out if Mr. Braun is busy."

The half-eggshell chair was a throwback to the sixties and just as uncomfortable. The girl was gone maybe a minute and when she came back the smile had been carefully replaced on her face.

"Mr. Braun will see you right away, sir. The second office to your left."

The door was open when I got there so I walked straight in. Sitting in back of the big executive desk was Eddie Braun, I guessed. Around thirty-five, with thick black hair, cold gray eyes, and he was wearing a sober dark suit. All in all, he looked about as glossy as his office furnishings. Standing slightly in back of him was a real big guy who looked like he would go around 220 pounds, even on a strict diet. He had wide sloping shoulders with thick slabs of muscle that seemed to keep right on going down to his wrists. His totally bald head was a bright pink color that didn't match with the faded blue of his eyes. Whenever you saw him coming you'd automatically step off the sidewalk without even thinking about it.

"Sit down, Mr. Holman," Braun said, and pointed toward a chair.

I sat down and gave him my polite attention.

"This is my associate," he said. "Mr. Olsen."

"Hi there, Mr. Olsen." I gave the hulk a big smile.

Olsen looked at me, shrugged his shoulders, then looked away again.

"I think I'll come straight to the point," Braun said, in a crisp-sounding voice. "Your reputation is known to me, Holman. A peeper with a sharp nose who's had a little luck in this town. It could run out if you try and play cute little games with me. Just what the hell is it you want?"

"I'm trying to find a girl."

"He sure fooled me," Olsen growled. "I had him figured for a fag."

"I don't think your associate is going to be much of a help, Mr. Braun," I said carefully. "Why don't you send him out to look for his hair, or something, while we talk?"

Olsen grunted and took a step toward me, then stopped when Braun waved a restraining hand.

"You have some specific girl in mind?" Braun asked.

"Gloria LaVerne," I said. "I think she was one of your rentagirls at one time. Maybe a year back?"

"You think she was one of my *what*?"

"Eddie, baby!" I shook my head slowly. "Your rentagirls are famous in this town. A hell of a lot more famous than your public relations outfit."

"I could drop him out the window," Olsen said. "It's four floors down. We could watch and see if he bounces."

"Gloria LaVerne," Braun repeated. "Who could ever forget a name like that? I never met any Gloria LaVerne."

"There's a guy called Pete, who's also interested in Gloria LaVerne," I said, then described him.

"No," Braun said. "I don't know any guy like that."

"Me, neither," Olsen volunteered unhelpfully.

"Then I guess you can't help me," I said, and got up onto my feet.

"Hold it," Braun said quickly. "One question before you go, Holman. Who pointed you at me?"

"My client's name is confidential."

"Maybe it wasn't your client."

"All my sources are confidential," I said smugly.

"I could tell Mike here to persuade you," he said. "Mike is real good at persuading people. Like he'll break off an arm and stuff it down your throat."

It was a morning when I had started out dressing right, so I was feeling real brave. I lifted the .38 out of the shoulder holster and hefted it in my hand.

"If he wants to try, I'll blow his head off," I said.

"He wouldn't dare use it," Olsen sneered.

I thumbed off the safety, aimed the gun and pulled the trigger. The shot sounded loud inside the confines of the office, then a small shower of plaster fell down onto Olsen's shoulder from a hole in the wall the slug had made about four inches away from the side of his head. The both of them stared at me numbly. I holstered the gun, gave them both a bright sunny smile of farewell and walked out of the office.

"Mr. Holman?" The receptionist looked very nervous indeed. "For a horrible moment back there I thought I heard the sound of a shot!"

"Don't worry about it," I told her. "It was only Mr. Olsen trying on a new toupee. Unfortunately he dropped it."

Her eyes were starting to revolve slowly as I headed toward the outer door.

There had to be a better way to handle things, I told myself when I got back to the car. I had made an enemy of Pete the previous night in the bar and he had been laying for me when I got home. Now I had made a couple more enemies out of Braun and Olsen. And so far I had learned exactly nothing about Gloria LaVerne. Or Alison Vaile, come to think of it. Maybe it was time I got into some other line of work? Or maybe it was time to do what I should have done in the first place; go talk with Alison Vaile. But it would be wise to check it out with my client first.

Her office was in West Hollywood and a walk-up on the third floor back. A cubbyhole pinch-hit as a reception area and a plump forty-year-old blonde gave me a suspicious stare as I walked in.

"Yes?" she said coldly.

"That's great!" I said enthusiastically. "I haven't had any sex today and it's almost noon already."

"What the hell are you talking about!"

"What do you care?" I said. "You already said yes!"

"A smart-ass!" she said. "And also an unknown

smart-ass. You want to get into pictures, sonny, you're around thirty years too late."

"That was when you were playing romantic leads, I bet!"

She grinned suddenly. "I can still play a few but they're more basic than romantic these days. Getting together all the sexual expertise I now have hasn't been easy."

"I'll believe it," I said. "I'm Rick Holman."

"I'm Maggie," she said. "I'm supposed to be the dragon-lady who scares the unwanted clients away. You don't scare easy, Mr. Holman."

"Maggie!" Sandy Parker's voice roared from the inner office. "You want to screw, screw on your own time. The same goes for idle chitchat!"

"I'll go tell her you heard okay but you were too busy screwing to answer," I said generously.

I walked past Maggie into the inner office and found Sandy Parker sitting in back of a large desk.

"It's you." Her lower lip curled. "I should have known."

She was wearing a brown suede coat and matching pants with a cream silk shirt underneath. A thin cheroot was held between the first two fingers of her right hand.

"I need to talk," I said.

"So talk," she said.

"Not with you," I said, "with Alison Vaile."

"I've been trying to call you for the last hour," she said. "Where the hell have you been?"

"Visiting with Eddie Braun."

"That panderer! I would have figured you could get your own girls, Holman."

"Alison Vaile must know what's bugging her," I said patiently. "Maybe she'll tell me, even if she won't tell you."

"Okay," Sandy said. "So talk with her."

"Fine."

"There's just one thing. You'll have to find her first."

"What the hell is that supposed to mean?"

"I got up late this morning," she said. "Alison had already gone. I checked out her room and most of her clothes had gone with her. No note, no sad good-bye written in lipstick on the mirror, no nothing. She got home early last night, looking like the sky had just fallen in, then went straight up to her room. I found her door locked on the inside when I went up later and she wouldn't answer when I called her name. So what did happen in the bar last night?"

I told her and the look on her face was even more sour by the time I had finished.

"You must be crazy!" she said. "I don't wonder she walked out on me this morning. You, a complete stranger, walking up to her table then knocking the guy she was with out cold. And then you had to go and call her Gloria LaVerne, for Christ's sake!"

"You don't have any idea where she might have gone?"

"How in hell could I?"

"I'm sorry I fouled it up for you," I said, speaking the words very carefully. "Good-bye, Sandy."

"Hold it!" she said harshly. "You don't walk out on me this easy, Holman. It's your fault she's gone, so it's up to you to bring her back."

"I'm not sure I'm that interested."

"You mean you figure it's too hard for your stupid

little brain to grapple with all on its own," she said. "You find her, Holman. You find out what all the big mystery is and you find out fast, or I'll blow so many holes in your reputation around this town you won't be able to get a job exercising poodles!"

"You're a great persuader, Sandy," I said. "Okay, I'll try. Incidentally, you owe me ninety bucks."

"Ninety dollars?" She bristled. "What the hell for?"

"Deposit on one of Eddie Braun's rentagirls," I said. "I wouldn't have bothered but she looks exactly like you."

Chapter 5

There were fifteen steps up to the front porch of the house in the Palisades. I rang the doorbell then checked my watch. It was one minute of six. Holman was nothing if not prompt. Nothing was starting to be a big thing in my life. I had spent all afternoon doing it. I should have been out looking for Alison Vaile but where the hell did I start? Then the front door opened and my train of thought was abruptly derailed.

She was someplace in her late twenties, I figured; tall, and generously built. Her strawberry-blonde hair was cut short and shaped to fit her skull like a cap. The large expressive eyes were a vivid blue and her mouth was wide and generous. She was wearing a full-length dress made from thin silk with large swirls of different colors overprinted. The material clung to her full hips and breasts and whispered whenever she moved.

"You're Holman?"

"And you're Sylvia Madden," I said.

"Come on in."

She turned and I followed her through the front hall into the living room. The funishings were all obviously products of the forties and gave the impression the room was a museum piece.

"It was the first house my late husband ever owned," she said. "His first wife furnished it in 1948. There doesn't seem to be any point in refurnishing. The way it is, it has a certain squalid charm about it, don't you think? It even has a cellaret that pops out of the wall. Reminds me of one of those oldfashioned private eyes who used to specialize in divorce." She gave me a wintry smile. "You don't specialize in divorce by any quaint chance, Mr. Holman?"

"Only when it features in somebody's background and could be important," I said. "Like Alison Vaile getting divorced from Duane Larsen."

"I checked you out again with Manny Kruger this afternoon just to be sure," she said. "I haven't made up my mind if I've forgiven him for giving you my unlisted number. Why don't you sit down, Mr. Holman, and what are you drinking?"

"Bourbon on the rocks, thanks," I told her, and sat down in a chintzy armchair.

I watched the cellaret pop out of the wall, curiously reminiscent of Groucho Marx, then she made the drinks. She brought mine over to me, then sat down facing me, her glass cradled in both hands.

"On the phone you said you wanted to talk about

Alison Vaile," she said. "I knew her at one time but she wasn't an intimate friend of mine."

"During the period she was married to Larsen and afterward?"

"They were divorced afterward, not long from the time I first met them. I saw Alison on occasions after that."

"She had three friends so Larsen told me," I said. "You, Eddie Braun, and Charles Stratton."

"And how is Duane these days? Still taking the straight route to death by alcoholic poisoning?"

I grinned. "Something like that."

"Tell me something, Mr. Holman." The vivid blue eyes watched me intently. "Just why are you so interested in Alison?"

I told her the the story about the television commercials Alison was refusing to do and how it worried her agent.

"Why don't you just ask Alison to tell you about her problem?"

"I would," I said, "but she's disappeared as of this morning. Moved out, taking her clothes with her."

"Where from?" she asked casually.

"Sandy Parker's house."

"Oh?" A fleeting smile showed up on her face. "She's been living with her agent. Now that's what I call real cozy."

"There's another woman involved in this someplace," I said. "Gloria LaVerne. Maybe you know her?"

Sylvia Madden's face became animated. "I've never met her but I sure have heard of her. She was a wild one, they said."

"They?"

"Charlie Stratton and Eddie Braun. At one time they almost never stopped talking about her. But I never seemed to get invited to the same parties she did. Then, after Louis Ashbury died, nobody talked about her anymore."

"Who was Louis Ashbury?"

"He and Charlie Stratton were kind of business partners, I think. He threw this fabulous party at his home in Bel Air one night then fell into the pool and drowned after everybody had gone home."

"And Gloria LaVerne was at the party?"

"She was at all the big parties." Sylvia Madden shrugged. "There was some kind of a scandal afterward involving her and Charlie. Then, like I said, I never heard her name mentioned again."

"Do you figure she was one of Eddie's rentagirls?"

"I wouldn't know."

"Tell me about Alison Vaile."

"I always figured Alison belonged on the Isle of Lesbos," she said. "And if she's been living with that well-known dyke, Sandy Parker, I guess it proves it. Alison seemed more relieved than anything else after she left Duane Larsen. For sure, he was a pig of a man to live with. He'd get blind drunk then beat up on her the whole time. I wonder why she stood it for as long as she did. After the divorce I didn't see her for a while. She was seeing Charlie and Eddie because they'd mention it to me. I was away in Europe for a while and when I came back she seemed to have dropped out of sight. Neither of them had seen her, either, they said."

"How long is it since Ashbury drowned?"

She thought for a few seconds. "Maybe a year back? No, more. It happened a few weeks before I went to Europe that time." She gave me a kind of coutesy smile. "I'm not being much help to you, Mr. Holman, I'm afraid."

"Where do I find Charlie Stratton?"

"Bel Air," she said. "You want to visit with him?"

"Right."

"Why don't we both go visit with him?" She licked her lower lip slowly. "In a weird kind of a way your investigation fascinates me, Mr. Holman. And Charlie is a real stuffed shirt. Sometimes I used to wonder about Alison's background, but Charlie is a true Brit right to his stuffy core. I swear he believes a penis is something you use to pee with!" Her smile was more genuine this time. "Do I shock you, Mr. Holman?"

"No."

"I'm glad about that. You have a car with you?"

"Sure. Don't you want to call Stratton and make sure he's home before we go visit him?"

"Charlie is strictly a man of dull routine," she said confidently. "At this time of day he'll be home and about halfway through his first martini."

I finished my drink as she collected her purse then we went out to the car. She gave me detailed instructions when we reached Bel Air, and finally we stopped in the driveway of one of those modest six-figure-bracket homes that grace the area. My convertible looked a little shabby parked beside the brand-new black Lincoln as we got out and walked up onto the front porch. Sylvia Madden pressed the doorbell and muted chimes played someplace inside the house.

"I think we should be friends, Rick," Sylvia Madden said suddenly. "Charlie will find it a little more reassuring that way. Please call me Sylvia."

"If we're going to be that friendly I figure it only fair to warn you I don't believe it's only for peeing with," I said.

She giggled, grabbed hold of my nearest hand and pressed it against the fullness of her right breast for a moment.

"I'm reassured," she said. "I was beginning to think you could be a fag."

She let go of my hand a couple of moments before the front door opened. The guy standing there with a dubious look on his face was around forty, I guessed. Tall, and almost gaunt-looking. His thinning black hair was brushed straight back across his head and his light blue eyes had a remote look to them. He was wearing an immaculately-tailored dark suit and a tie overprinted with significant little emblems. For all I could tell the little emblems were nipples and he was a founding member of the boob-fanciers club.

"Hellow, Sylvia," he said, in a clipped, very English, accent.

"Hello, Charlie," she said brightly. "This is a great friend of mine, Rick Holman."

"How d'you do," Stratton said, with no warmth at all.

"Rick's investigating a fascinating problem all to do with dear Alison Vaile," Sylvia went on at a fast clip. "I just knew you'd be fascinated, too, and what better time for us to drop in than martini-time?"

Stratton didn't look enchanted, exactly. "Yes, well—" he cleared his throat a couple of times. "If it doesn't take too long. I have an engagement later this evening."

We followed him into the house. The living room

was spacious; the furniture was fake colonial, and a row of hunting prints hung along one wall. There was no sign of any feminine influence at all.

"Please sit down," Stratton said stiffly. "You'll have a martini, Mr. Holman?"

"Thanks," I said.

He got two goblets out of a cabinet, put them on the silver tray, and poured the drinks from the silver shaker. His own glass was half-empty, I noticed, which said something for Sylvia's timing. Then he brought the drinks across to the couch which Sylvia and I were sharing.

"Tell Charlie all about it," Sylvia commanded.

So I told him the story about Alison Vaile and how it seemed important to find out what had happened to her during the year after she had been divorced from Duane Larsen.

"Can't help you much," he said, when I had finished. "Saw her from time to time, you know. She seemed to be surviving all right. Reticent about what she was doing and I didn't like to pry. Sorry I can't be more specific than that, Holman."

"There's something else," Sylvia said quickly. "Rick thinks there's another woman involved. Gloria LaVerne."

"Oh?" Stratton sipped his martini delicately. "Why is that?"

"Her name keeps on getting mentioned," I said vaguely.

"And she used to go to all those wild parties you and Eddie told me about," Sylvia said. "And wasn't there some scandal about her after Louis Ashbury's party. You know, the night he drowned in his own pool?"

"I don't recall any," Stratton said. "She achieved some notoriety with her behavior at parties. I seem to recall one time when she stripped off all her clothes and cavorted naked in somebody's pool.

"What did she look like?" I asked him.

"Hard to say." He chewed on his lower lip for a moment. "One time you'd see her she was a blonde. The next time, a redhead. The time after that, a brunette. I presume they were all wigs, of course. But she did have a magnificent body. I remember seeing her at quite close quarters the time she dived naked into the pool." He shook his head slowly. "A really magnificent body!"

"You old dog!" Sylvia said triumphantly. "And just how close to that magnificent body did you get?"

"Not that close," he snapped. "It was rumored she was freely available but the price was very high. I'm not interested in that sort of thing."

"Louis Ashbury was your partner," I said.

"Sylvia does seem to have been confiding in you, Holman." He have her a steely glare. "Yes, he was, as a matter of fact. If his death hadn't been so tragic it would have seemed quite idiotic. To drown in one's own swimming pool!"

"You were at the party that night?"

"Oh, yes." He nodded. "I left when most of the other people there were leaving. Sometime around three A.M. I should imagine."

"And Gloria LaVerne was there?"

"As I recall." He nodded again. "She was a brunette that time, I think."

"Just what kind of partnership were you and Ashbury in?"

"I can't see how that could possibly be relevant to

your enquiries about Alison Vaile," he said coldly. "However, it's no secret. We were concerned with investment. Wild-cat investment is the American term for it, I think? In other words, the kind of investment no bank or finance house would touch with a forty-foot pole. You take a high risk, but if the investment pays off you stand to make a high profit."

"And if it doesn't pay off?"

He smiled bleakly. "You lick your wounds and hope the next one will be better."

"Something like Eddie Braun's 'Media-On,' would be high risk," I said easily. "Do you have a piece of his action, Mr. Stratton?"

"I consider the question an outrageous impertience," he said. "Do you have any more questions, Holman? Reasonable questions, that is. As I mentioned before I do have this previous appointment."

"You've been very helpful, Mr. Stratton," I told him.

"I just knew you'd be absolutely fascinated, Charlie," Sylvia said enthusiastically. "Anytime you want somebody with a magnificent body to dive naked into your pool at one of your parties, you just call me."

"Good-bye, Sylvia," he said, then nodded distantly in my direction. "Holman."

He didn't bother seeing us out. We got back into the car and wheeled down the gravel driveway, past all the pristine shrubs and flowers. I wouldn't have been surprised to see a sign which said, "No bees allowed."

"I told you he was a stuffed shirt," Sylvia said, as we reached the road. "I was wrong about that. More like a stuffed prick!"

"He's not married?"

She laughed. "Can you imagine Charlie being married? Charlie is a cold fish most of the time but he breaks out on occasion. Then he's a real kink!"

"To know Charlie, is to not love Charlie," I said wisely.

"You sank a knife into him about 'Media-On,' for sure," she said. "It's funny, I used to wonder how a couple of guys like him and Eddie Braun could ever be friends. They're completely different in just about everything. But if Charlie has a piece of Eddie's action that could explain it."

"And how about Gloria LaVerne," I said. "The girl with the magnificent body and a head full of surprises?"

"Ringing the changes with her full set of wigs," Sylvia said, then shook her head slowly. "How corny can you get!"

"Does Charlie throw many parties?"

"Not many," she said. "When he does, they're usually good ones. When his kinks start to break out all over, that's the time Charlie throws a party."

"How about Eddie Braun?"

"Eddie doesn't throw parties," she said. "He's too busy supplying the necessary ingredients for other people's parties. Like girls are his specialty."

"Rentagirls," I said. "I wonder if Gloria LaVerne worked for him."

"Highly probable, I'd figure." She leaned back against the upholstery and sighed gently. "I'd guess we weren't a big social success with Charlie. It's a lousy way to start an evening. We should improve on it, Rick. Do you have any plans for the rest of the night?"

"I was thinking of throwing a party at my place," I said. "A very limited number of guests. Then I was going to call and ask you to come on over and display your magnificent body naked when you dive into my pool."

"You have a pool?"

"An itty-bitty one," I admitted.

"How many people were you figuring on inviting, exactly?"

I thought about it for a couple of seconds. "Two."

"It sounds like my kind of a party," she said. "But why don't we have it at my place?"

"Do you have a pool?"

"Just a magnificent body," she said complacently. "Will that do?"

"It'll do just fine," I said. "So long as you don't mind me diving straight into it."

I nearly collected a truck beside me in the inside lane a couple of seconds later when her hand crept up the inside of my thigh right into my crotch, then two fingers nipped fiercely.

"You should keep your mind on your driving," she said demurely, as the sound of the outraged horn had finally faded in back of us.

"And you should keep your zipper-plucking fingers to yourself," I told her.

"And only half-erect," she murmured. "It was almost an insult."

We got back to her house in the Palisades and climbed the fifteen steps up to her front porch.

"You want to make us a drink," she said, when we reached the living room. "I'm going to the kitchen and start preparing dinner. 'Never had sex on an empty stomach,' my old grannie used to say to me, and ever afterward I've always been worried about if the guy I'm with has eaten."

"Was that the problem with the late Benjamin Madden?" I asked her. "I mean, was it sex on an empty stomach that gave him that coronary occlusion?"

She shook her head slowly. "I guess Ben had it coming, the way we all have it coming, sooner or later. In his own kind of way, Ben was a very nice guy. He liked women and he was old-fashioned enough to believe he should marry them before he screwed them."

"I'm sorry," I said. "It was a kind of cheap question, at that."

"Everybody believes I married him for his money," she said, "and they're right. I never made any secret of it. Ben knew it. But I didn't screw him to death. He had one attack before the second fatal one, and I nursed him like a mother hen for three months. It was the least I could do. The nearest we came to sex in all that time was one night when he slipped his hand inside my blouse and fondled one of my breasts. Just to make sure his memories were real, he said."

"Why is it nobody ever lives up to their reputation?" I said bitterly. "Now you seem like a nice lady."

The dinner was superb, both the food and imported wine the kind of experience a bachelor finds rare in his sordid life of meals mostly grabbed in diners and chicken inns. Afterward, we went back into the living room.

"You'll stay the night, of course," Sylvia said easily.

"One thing I really appreciate," I said, "and that's your wild impetuous romantic approach."

She grinned. "That was another thing my old grannie used to say; never make love straight after a big meal because just one burp in the wrong place could ruin a man for life."

The phone rang and she pulled a face before she answered it. Her answers tended to be monosyllabic and grew more terse the whole time until she finally said, "And fuck you, Charlie!" then hung up.

"That was Charlie," she said bleakly as she came back to the couch.

"I would never have guessed," I said.

"Charlie is mad at me for taking you along to his place earlier tonight. When Charlie is mad he forgets he's pretending to be a gentleman and you have to talk to him in the four-letter kind of words he understands."

"Is that right?" I said politely.

"Charlie says you are dangerous and it was very stupid of me to take you to his house and if I ever do anything like that again, I'll regret it."

"He'll put you over his knee?"

"More like send his old buddy, Eddie Braun, around to visit," she said slowly. "Eddie is real good at that kind of thing. He's had a lot of practice."

"Why do you figure Charlie is so worried about me?"

"I don't know." She shrugged. "Maybe because, like I said before, you seemed to hit a vein when you suggested he could be backing Eddie Braun."

"When his partner drowned in the pool," I said. "It was an accident?"

She stared at me for a long moment, her vivid blue

eyes widening. "Why do you ask that?"

"I'm just curious."

"Everybody figured it was an accident, including the coroner. Ashbury was so drunk he must have fallen into his pool and drowned. The alcoholic content of his blood was like right off the scale, they said.

"And Gloria LaVerne was at the party along with Charlie and Eddie," I said.

"Just who is this Gloria LaVerne, anyway?"

"I don't know. Her name keeps coming up the whole time and maybe she was a friend of Alison's, too. There's also a guy called, Pete, who is a friend of hers. Maybe you know him?"

I gave her a detailed description of Pete and she shook her head firmly.

"I don't know anybody like that," she said. "And from the way you describe him, I'm glad."

"You have any idea where Alison Vaile might have gone after she left Sandy Parker's house?"

She thought about it for a little time. "She wouldn't go back to Duane Larsen, that's for sure, and I figure she wasn't at Charlie's house, either, when we visited. Charlie's house is so goddamned masculine and sterile, you could tell if a woman had even set foot inside the place."

"Eddie Braun?"

"I doubt that. Even when they were friends, Alison seemed to be scared of being in the same room with him, most of the time. It was only because he was a friend of Duane's that she tolerated him, I guess."

"Duane seemed to think Braun was a good friend of hers."

"Then Duane is stupid," she said. "Right?"

"I'm not sure about that," I said. "With him, it's real hard to see past the gunfighter image."

"I am beginning to get bored with this conversation, Rick," she said. "And I'm still irritated with Charlie Stratton. Who the hell does he think he is, calling me like that!"

She got up from the couch and moved across to the window and stood there with her back toward me.

"How is your digestive tract?" she asked suddenly.

"Purring. How's yours?"

"Functioning perfectly," she said. "So maybe now is the time, like my old grannie used to say."

"What was your old grannie?" I asked her. "A hooker?"

"She was the madame of a brothel in Pessary, Ohio," Sylvia said casually. "On her days off she used to fill in for one of the girls. Just to keep her hand in, she said. Along with the rest of her equipment, of course."

One hand reached up behind her back and unzipped the full-length dress so it collapsed in a soft heap around her ankles. Underneath, she was wearing white silk briefs that clung tight to her hips. A light golden tan covered the rest of her. She stepped out of the dress and turned around toward me. Her full breasts stood free, contemptuously ignoring gravity, and the large plum-colored nipples began to harden in the coolness of the air-conditioned room. It was one hell of a moment for the doorbell to ring.

"Oh, shit!" Sylvia said helplessly.

"We could just ignore it until whoever it is goes away," I suggested.

She shook her head. "I guess I'd better find out who it is, Rick. Your car is parked right out front so they'll know I'm home."

She picked up her dress and climbed back into it. "Zip me up, please."

The doorbell rang again as I closed the zip.

"And did the earth move for you?" she said, and giggled suddenly. "That's got to be about the fastest non-event in the whole history of sex. Get yourself a drink while I see if I can get rid of whoever it is who's ruining our sex life."

I went over to the cellaret as she left the room and made myself a small brandy. The memory of her bare breasts seemed to be engraved on the front of my mind in absolute detail. Maybe thirty seconds later she came back into the room closely followed by Eddie Braun and Mike Olsen.

"Suddenly, it seems like I'm always meeting you, Holman," Braun said.

"Maybe it's because we only know the best people," I said.

Olsen's faded blue eyes looked at me with innate contempt, then a gun appeared in his hand a moment later.

"The last time you got real cute," he said. "So this time you take the gun out real slow with two fingers and drop it on the floor."

There was no percentage in arguing with him. I eased the .38 out of the holster, using just the two fingers, and dropped it onto the floor.

"Now kick it over here," he said.

I did like he said and he bent down to pick up the

gun. Then he holstered his own gun.

"Just what is all this about?" Sylvia demanded.

"You got a big mouth," Braun told her. "You open it too wide to the wrong people." He pointed a finger at me. "Like him."

"I'll talk with whoever I like," she said. "Who do you think you are, busting into my house like this and—"

He hit her. A vicious slap across the side of her face and the staccato sound was like a gunshot. She went staggering for maybe a half-dozen steps then regained her balance. The imprint of Braun's hand was etched in angry red against the whiteness of her cheek.

"Rick?" There was a hoarse emotional appeal in her voice.

I got up onto my feet and Olsen grinned broadly at me, as he made a quick beckoning gesture with his right hand.

"Come on and try your luck, Holman," he said. "Your face could do with some rearranging."

He had a weight advantage of around fifty pounds, I figured, and it was mostly muscle. Going up against Olsen had about as much future as Fay Wray would have had taking a swipe at King Kong. So I sat down again and the frozen look on Sylvia's face said the age of chivalry had just died all over again.

"Holman's coming with us," Braun said. "Something I want him to see. Just keep your fat lip closed in future, honey."

Sylvia opened her mouth to say something, suddenly changed her mind, and closed it again.

"Okay." Braun looked at me. "Let's go. You can

drive your own car and Mike will keep you company."

I got up onto my feet again and headed toward the door. The two of them walked real close in back of me. I had the feeling Sylvia was in no mood for a fond farewell, so I didn't give her one. Anyway, I figured, for her right now, a non-hero was strictly a non-event.

Chapter 6

It was a shack way up in the hills. It had taken over an hour's drive to reach it. I parked my car alongside Braun's, then got out. Olsen joined me a moment later and we walked up the four wooden stairs onto the verandah. Braun unlocked the front door and then we went inside. He switched on the lights and I saw we were in a large living room with plain, but adequate, furniture.

"It's my little hideaway in the hills," Braun said. "The nearest neighbor is a half-mile away and then it's only a summer place." He walked over to the bar and started making himself a drink. "It has advantages. No phone, no interruptions, and somebody could scream their head off with no hope of being heard at all."

"What do you want from me?" I asked him.

"You've got nothing I want, Holman," he said.

"You're just a goddamned irritant. Sticking your nose where it doesn't belong. Talking to my friends and clients."

"Why don't I break his nose for him?" Olsen said. "Just for starters."

"Don't be rude to our guest, Mike," Braun said easily. "Talking of guests, I figure he should meet our other guest. Why don't you bring her in for a moment?"

Olsen nodded, then walked out of the room. Braun sipped his drink and watched me with a faint smile on his face. Maybe a minute later, Olsen was back with a stark-naked Julie for company. Her eyes were puffed and swollen, and her straight dark hair fell down around her face. There were dark bruises on the undersides of her breasts and across her stomach.

"Turn around, baby," Braun said, "and let Holman get the full picture."

She turned around slowly until her back was toward me. Livid weals stood out in horizontal stripes across the fullness of her bottom and the tops of her thighs. She had been beaten very badly and by an expert who had just stopped short of doing her any permanent damage.

"Okay," Braun said. "That's enough. Take her back now."

Olsen put one massive hand on her shoulder and propelled her out of the room.

"You went and visited with one of my clients," Braun said. "He said he told you nothing and I believe him. But somebody told you about my rentagirls, Holman. Who else, but the rentagirl he had with him?"

"You're taking a lot of trouble about this, Eddie," I said. "I keep on wondering why, exactly?"

"It's no trouble," he said. "Mike figures it's a pleasure."

Olsen came back into the room, closing the door carefully in back of him.

"She said she's cold in there," he said amiably. "I offered to warm her ass for her all over again and that took care of it."

Braun finished his drink and put the empty glass down onto the bartop. "It's like this, Holman," he said. "You're out of your league. I don't want you sticking your nose into my affairs, my friends' affairs, or my clients' affairs. You can take this as a mild kind of warning. If you ignore it, you're going to wind up dead."

He walked across to the door and opened it, then looked back over his shoulder.

"When you're all through here, Mike," he said. "I'll see you back in the city."

The door closed in back of him and I moved quickly behind the bar.

"I need a drink," I said, and set up a glass.

"You don't have time for a drink, Holman," Olsen said. "Get your clothes off."

"What?"

"You heard me." He grinned at me, an almost loving expression in his eyes. "You saw the broad. You get the same treatment. It's a warning, the boss said. It'll hurt like hell but I'll make sure I don't do any permanent damage. A few days and you'll be as good as new. Well, almost." He chuckled at the thought. "So quit fooling around and get your goddamned clothes off!"

"I told you," I said, "I need a drink."

I lifted the bottle Braun had used and poured a generous measure into the glass. There was a dull gleam in Olsen's faded blue eyes as he watched me. Then he took out his gun and pointed it at me.

"You got three seconds to start stripping, Holman," he said, in a flat voice.

"You need a gun to take me?" I grinned derisively at him. "You won't use it, Mike. Your boss said no permanent damage. I'm surprised you're scared of me. A great big fag like you shouldn't be be scared of anybody, except women!"

His face darkened with fury and he made a sharp grunting noise. Then he came straight at me. The bar wasn't about to get in his way, I realized. He was going to come straight over it, or straight through it, to get at me. That crack about him being a fag had sunk home. When he got real close I tossed the contents of my glass into his face and the neat whisky searing his eyeballs slowed him down for a moment. Then I grabbed the near-full bottle by the neck and swung it in a tight arc until it hit him on the side of the head. It made a dull crunching sound and the jarring impact nearly made me drop the bottle, but I didn't. He made another grunting sound and shook his head. This time I slammed the bottle down on top of his head and the impact drove him onto his knees. I hit him again in the same place and the massive bulk of him slid sideways onto the floor. There was no way of knowing if I had killed him and, right then, I didn't give a goddamn either way.

I moved around the bar fast and kneeled down beside him. He was still breathing, slowly and heavily, and his face was a dull gray color. I retrieved my gun and his gun. My own gun I put back into the empty shoulder-holster and his gun I shoved into my hip pocket. Then I made myself a fresh drink and drank it neat in two gulps. Sudden warmth exploded in my belly a few seconds later and I began to feel better. From the look of Olsen he was going to be out cold for some time to come. I resisted the urge to kick him in the head for all the plans he had for me. Instead, I stripped off all his clothes and left him lying naked on the floor. Most of his body was covered with a pelt of dark fur which maybe compensated for his baldness, but also made him look completely inhuman, more like some primordial beast out of the forest. Then I went looking for Julie.

There were two bedrooms and a bathroom, besides the kitchen. One of the bedroom doors was locked so I kicked it in. It was Holman's night for violence, I figured. When the door sprang open, I switched on the light and saw Julie cowering in one corner with her hands over her face.

"Last car back to the city is leaving in a couple of minutes," I told her.

She slowly took her hands away from her face and stared at me in disbelief.

"Rick?" Her voice shook. "Oh, my God! I can't believe it."

"What did they do with your clothes?"

"I don't know." She shook her head helplessly.

"Maybe they're in the other bedroom," I said. "Go look, then join me in the living room."

"What about the others?"

"Braun left," I said. "Olsen's still here but he's not interested in anything right now."

I went back into the living room and made myself another drink. A sudden generous impulse made me set up one for Julie, as well. Time seemed to drag by with the only sound in the room the ragged harshness of Olsen's unsteady breathing, then Julie appeared. She was wearing a dress and carrying her purse, walking slowly and painfully like a very old woman.

"I made you a drink," I said, and held out the glass to her.

"Thanks." She took it from me then looked down at Olsen. "Is he dead?"

"I don't think so," I told her.

"What happened?"

"I clobbered him with a bottle," I said. "The idea was for me to strip off all my clothes, then he was going to give me the same treatment he'd given you. Afterward, I guess he was going to use my car to get back to the city and leave the both of us here."

She shuddered. "He's a sadist!"

"He's also a fag," I said. "I guess that kind of combination makes him real useful to Braun to control his rentagirls. Or it did."

"Did?" She looked at me nervously.

"Depends on how hard his skull is," I said. "I could have scrambled his brains permanently."

"It doesn't worry you?"

"Are you kidding?" I gaped at her. "After what he did to you, and what he planned on doing to me?"

"It's funny," she said. "When I first met you I wondered what a nice guy like you was doing in your line of work. Now I know."

"Finish your drink and we'll get out of here, to coin a phrase," I said.

She finished her drink but she was still shivering. It

was a warm night but after what she had been through I figured she hadn't noticed it yet. I picked up the pile of Olsen's clothing and took it with me out to the car. The keys were still in the dash which didn't make life any more complicated. Julie sat beside me in the passenger's seat and I started the motor.

"Are they Olsen's clothes?" She looked over her shoulder at the pile on the back seat.

"That's right."

"What are you going to do with them?"

"Toss them into the bushes someplace about three miles down the road."

"You mean you're just going to leave him there, unconscious and naked, all his own?"

"Damned right."

She started to giggle suddenly. "My God!" she said, in an explosive gasp. "Now I'm beginning to be as bad as you. You want to know something? I like it! I hope a huge swarm of bees settle on him before he wakes up, too!"

I stopped the car a couple of miles down the road and tossed the clothes into the nearest clump of bushes, remembering to extract the wallet beforehand. Then I drove on. Beside me, Julie suddenly clutched my arm.

"I forgot to say thank you," she said. "So, thank you."

"It was almost a pleasure."

"There's one other thing just occurred to me," she said. "What the hell do I do now?"

"Where do you live?"

"West Hollywood."

"Why don't we go straight there? You can pick up some more clothes and then come back to my place."

She shifted uncomfortably in her seat.

"It doesn't appeal to you?" I queried.

"It's not that," she said. "It's like sitting on red hot coals!"

"If you prefer to stay at your place, I can let you have Olsen's gun," I said generously.

"No," she said sharply. "I much prefer to stay at your place, Rick. Thank you."

"Don't keep thanking me."

"Okay, so I un-thank you."

"That Olsen," I said. "Just looking at him kind of shrivels up any milk of human kindness you might have left."

"What will happen if he dies?"

"I guess they'll bury him, eventually," I said indifferently.

That did up the conversation just fine for the next half-hour. It was close to midnight when I parked outside the apartment block in West Hollywood. I sat in the car and waited while Julie collected her clothes. She came back, lugging a suitcase, around a half-hour later. Like all women she had instant decision when it came to clothes, I guessed. Twenty minutes later we were back at my house in Beverly Hills.

I took the suitcase into the bedroom and came back to find Julie standing in the center of the living room.

"Why don't you sit down and relax," I suggested.

"The one thing I can't do when I sit down is relax," she said tartly. "I told you before in the car."

"It's a shame," I said. "A cigar is only a smoke, but a girl's beautiful bottom is a joy forever."

"Oh, shit!" she said despairingly.

"Do you want a drink?"

"I want to take a very careful shower," she said. "And there's another thing, Rick Holman. I'm hungry."

"So go take your shower and I'll get you something to eat," I said.

She headed toward the bathroom and I headed toward the kitchen. I found a steak in the refrigerator and a pack of frozen French fries. It was the kind of gourmet meal I'm an expert in preparing. I went back to the bar and made a bourbon on the rocks to keep the chef company while he was working, then returned to the kitchen again. The food was just about ready when Julie stuck her head around the door.

"It smells good," she said.

"Go back to the living room and help yourself to a drink," I said. "Another couple of minutes and I'll bring it it."

She was standing in the center of the room again when I brought in the tray, wearing a shirt that just reached the tops of her thighs.

"Clothes hurt," she said, "Especially pants because they fit real tight and they cling. I only mention the fact so you won't get any wrong ideas, Holman. The thought of sex right now rates with me on about the same scale as beating my head against a brick wall."

I thoughtfully put the tray on the bartop so she could eat standing up. The thought of a long leisurely shower seemed like a good idea, and it was better than just standing there and watching her eat. I told Julie what I was about to do and she showed a singular lack of interest in between making steady chomping sounds. I took my drink to the bathroom with me.

Maybe fifteen minutes later I was all dried off and everything. I was also tired, I realized, and there was no point in putting on any clothes just to take them off again a couple of minutes later. So I walked into the bedroom wearing only the glass in my right hand, and saw I had been beaten to it. Julie was sprawled across the bed on her stomach and had obviously discarded her shirt.

"Hi." She looked up at me over her shoulder. "I was wondering if you'd do me a small favor, Rick?"

"Like what?"

"I've got this jar of cold cream with me," she said. "I've done my front and it helps but I can't manage my back. Would you mind doing it for me?"

"Sure," I said.

I put my glass down on the bedside table and picked up the jar of cold cream. The question was, where to start? Start at the beginning and go onto the end, I figured cleverly was the answer. The end in question with all those weals across it looked very vulnerable indeed. I placed a hunk of goo on the top curve of the lefthand cheek of her bottom and began to rub it in gently with a circular movement of my fingers.

"So what happened?" I asked her.

"From where you're sitting I would have figured it was obvious," she said coldly.

"I mean, with Braun and Olsen."

"They came to visit with Duane Larsen," she said. "I listened behind the door. Duane was drunk, but not stupid drunk. He said, sure you'd visited with him but he hadn't told you anything. So then they figured it had to be me. They just grabbed hold of me and hustled me out to the car. Duane was a real hero. He just stood there, looking the other way and pretending it wasn't happening. They drove me out to that shack in the hills and made me strip off my clothes. I was so scared I told them everything I'd told you which wasn't that much, but Braun said I had to be taught a lesson. Then Olsen took me into one of the bedrooms and started to beat me." She shivered involuntarily. "It hurt, Rick! For a time there I figured he was going to kill me. He was enjoying it so much."

I dropped another hunk of goo onto the roundest curve of the left-hand cheek and massaged it into the warm flesh. It could be one hell of a way to make a living, I thought idly.

"That helps," Julie said. "It's very soothing."

"What time was it when they picked you up from Larsen's house?"

"Around three this afternoon."

They had known exactly where to find me later, I remembered. For sure, Sylvia hadn't told them. So it figured they'd had a call from Charlie Stratton. Then I also remembered Braun saying there was no phone at the shack. I went on automatically massaging the goo into her flesh until both cheeks of her buttocks were covered with a fine sheen. Julie gave a contented sigh and spread her legs apart, revealing a tuft of springy black pubic heair between their tops. The fingers of my right hand seemed to suddenly acquire a life of their own. They slipped down between the tops of her legs and gently stroked, finding a yielding warm dampness there.

"I knew it was going to happen," Julie murmured. "Now I feel horny as hell!"

I looked down at my erect shaft waving hopefully in the air and said, "So is your masseur."

"But how?" she said desperately.

"Love will find a way," I said confidently. "The problem is, which way?"

My fingers kept right on stroking and her vaginal lips surrendered moistly and I gently squeezed her enlarge clitoris. Suddenly she brought her knees up under her, raising her bottom into the air, while her head pressed into the cushions.

"This way," she said, in a muffled voice. "But gently, please, Rick."

I eased my shaft slowly into the intimate haven and, as it sank fully home, the base of my stomach bounced against the soft cheeks of her bottom. Julie let out a stifled yelp and I would have withdrawn in sympathy, but her vaginal muscles clamped tight around my shaft.

"Never mind the yelps," she said, in the same muffled voice.

They were her yelps, I figured, and if she said not to mind, then I wouldn't mind. One sudden more violent yelp heralded the beginning of her orgasm and mine quickly followed. And when it was all over she lay flat on her stomach again and made purring noises of contentment.

"Is there any cold cream left?" she asked.

"Sure," I said.

"Well, don't just sit there," she said. "Start massaging!"

Chapter 7

Julie served breakfast in the morning like it was beginning to be a habit. She wore the same shirt she had worn the previous night and it was distracting.

"You were nice to me last night, Rick," she said. "I wanted to thank you."

"The same goes for you, too," I told her. "How are you feeling this morning?"

"Still sore, but a hell of a lot better than I felt locked in that bedroom." She went to sit down then changed her mind quickly. "What happens now?"

"I'll have some more coffee, thanks."

"I mean for the rest of today, and then tomorrow, and after that the day after."

"I figure I'll have to take Eddie Braun apart," I said. "Either that, or he'll take me apart."

"I don't find that comforting, exactly."

"You've got a choice," I said. "You can stay here

with me and hope I win, or you can pack your bag and leave town."

"I like it here," she said. "Where else can you get smog and oranges anytime you want?"

"You stay here, I'll leave you Olsen's gun," I said. "You don't answer the doorbell and you don't answer the phone unless it's me. If it's me, I'll let the phone ring three times, hang up, then dial again immediately."

"You'll have to leave me alone here, I realize that," she said. "Will I be safe, Rick?"

"No," I said honestly. "If anybody, including Braun, wants to bust in here the locks won't stop them."

She thought about it for a few seconds then grinned at me ruefully. "I couldn't use a gun," she said, "not under any circumstances, Rick. In theory I could shoot somebody like Mike Olsen, but in reality I know I couldn't. Not when it came to the point of pulling the trigger."

"I can't stay home the whole time," I said gently.

"Then I guess it has to be a big farewell to the smog and the oranges," she said. "I think I'm going to miss you, Rick."

"Where will you go?"

"Back home for a while, I guess. That's Oregon. I haven't been back in a couple of years."

"You have family there?"

She nodded. "My parents, and my sister, who is married to a creep but doesn't know it."

"How about money?"

"No problem," she said. "I've saved most of what I've made out of being a rentagirl. Maybe I'll settle down in Oregon and get myself a legitimate job, or even get married. Who knows?"

"I'd like you to stay," I said. "You know that."

"You're an exciting man to make love with, Rick," she said. "Even when it hurts. But yesterday gave me a taste of the kind of world you live in, and I'm just not equipped for it." She smiled again, almost shyly. "I scare easy!"

"You want to drive you to your apartment and help you pack?" I asked.

"No, thanks. You can call me a cab while I get dressed is all. You've done enough for me already, Rick."

She leaned forward and kissed me gently on the forehead. "That's for good-bye."

"And you didn't even yelp," I said.

The cab picked her up around twenty minutes later and she gave me a quick bright smile as she went past me and out the front door. California's loss would be Oregon's gain, I figured, as I watched the cab accelerate down the driveway and disappear out onto the street. The house seemed a bleak kind of place to be in after I had closed the front door and went back to the living room. I retrieved Olsen's wallet and emptied out the contents. A driving license, a string of credit cards and around a couple of hundred dollars in cash. Nothing personal, and no vital clues emerged. Then the phone rang.

"I figured there had to be something wrong so I went back," Eddie Braun's voice had a brittle quality to it. "Got up to the shack around two this morning. Mike's in the hospital. They tell me the concussion is real bad and they don't know how he'll be when he comes out of it. *If* he comes out of it."

"Tough," I said.

"Whatever happens to Mike, I'm going to kill you, Holman," Braun said. "I just want you to know that."

Then he hung up. I checked out Larsen's number and dialed it. The phone rang for a long time before anybody answered it.

"Mr. Larsen's residence," a cautious-sounding female voice said.

Come hell or high water, I guessed the rentagirl system kept right on functioning.

"This is Rick Holman," I said. "I'd like to speak with Mr. Larsen."

"I'm sorry, he's not awake yet. Maybe if you called back sometime this afternoon."

"It's urgent I see him," I said. "Tell him I can stop what happened to Julie from ruining his chances of a big new movie with Stellar. I'll be there in around an hour and have him give me clearance with the gate people."

"But—" she said, the moment before I hung up.

I dialed Stellar and asked to be put through to Manny Kruger. There was the usual delays and clunking sounds, then Liz Moody's voice said, "Mr. Kruger's office."

"It's Rick Holman," I said.

"The man with all that pulsating energy going to waste," she said. "Have you been violent again?"

"Not since last night," I told her truthfully.

"If you channeled it where it belongs, like someplace between your legs," she said thoughtfully. "You'd be insatiable. Have you ever thought about that?" Then, before I could dream up an answer, her voice became strictly professional. "Oh, Mr. Kruger. I have Mr. Holman for you on line one."

"Let me know when you've got a spare week coming up and we can test out your theory," I said.

She gave a kind of wanton snort, there was a clicking sound, then Manny Kruger's voice boomed in my ear.

"I was just about to call you, Rick," he said. "I saw Larsen yesterday."

"And?" I said encouragingly.

"When I started to talk about the remake of 'The Hunchback of Notre Dame,' he acted like I was crazy, or something!"

"You scared the hell out of him," I said quickly. "The fact that you knew about it fazed him completely."

There was a long silence and pregnant wasn't a strong enough word for it.

"That's the way you see it," Manny said finally.

"Sure," I said confidently. "Look, I'm going to see him myself in a little while. I'll push him into admitting it then tell him the only chance he's got of making the movie is to rely entirely on you."

"You'll do that for me, Rick?" Manny couldn't believe it.

"Anything for an old buddy," I said expansively.

"You're the best, Rick!" He breathed heavily into the phone for a few seconds to make sure I understood how he felt.

"Maybe you can help me, too, Manny," I said.

"You want a percentage of the motion picture!" he almost screamed.

"Just some information. You know everybody in this town, Manny, my old buddy."

"Like who, out of everybody, do you want to know about?"

"Charlie Stratton."

"What's with Charlie Stratton?"

"You tell me."

"Veddy English," Manny said. "Sometimes he's so goddamned English, I wonder if he's a phoney. A kind of wildcat investor. When you can't get money any other place and you're real desperate you go to Charlie Stratton."

"He had a partner one time, right?"

"Lou Ashbury." His voice was cautious again. "So what?"

"He died."

"Got smashed out of his mind at one of his own parties and drowned in his own pool," Manny said. "Just over a year back as I remember. Why do you care?"

"Idly curious," I said.

"This doesn't have anything to do with Duane Larsen?"

"Absolutely nothing," I said. "I'm trying to find a girl who used to go to a lot of parties around that time. She was there at Ashbury's party that night."

"A lot of girls go to parties," he said. "She has a name?"

"Gloria LaVerne."

He cackled suddenly. "She wasn't a star of the silent screen, or something?"

"You never heard of her?"

"A name like that, I'd remember."

"I guess you're right," I said reluctantly.

"Let me know how things go with Larsen, okay, old buddy?"

"Sure, old buddy," I said.

One more call before I ventured out into the wild,

85

wild world. Sylvia Madden's voice sounded remote when she answered her phone.

"Rick Holman," I said.

"Are you still alive?"

"Olsen is in the hospital and Eddie Braun's mad at me," I said.

"You expect me to believe that?"

"There's no way you can go up against a guy built the way Olsen is in a sporting fashion with your fists raised," I said. "He'll beat the hell out of you with one hand. You need an edge."

"What kind of an edge?" Her voice was sarcastic.

"A near-full bottle of Scotch will do," I said. "Something you can beat his head in with. I didn't have one at your place."

"Is that what you did to him last night? Beat his head in with a near-full bottle of Scotch?"

"It felt good," I said. "Like something Olsen's been needing for a long time."

"In a weird kind of a way I find myself believing you," she said.

"I have to see you."

"Tonight," she said. "I'm supposed to be having dinner at Charlie Stratton's place, but the hell with him."

"What time?"

"Around eight. But if we have any interruptions this time, I expect you to take care of them right away, Rick Holman. Near-full bottle of Scotch, or no near-full bottle of Scotch!"

"I'll see you," I said.

I pulled up at the steel mesh barrier just off Benedict Canyon and waited. One of the uniformed private cops sauntered across and stared at me through the mesh.

"Holman," I said. "To see Mr. Larsen. I'm expected."

"Sure thing, Mr. Holman." He waved to his buddy inside the guardhouse and the barrier began to pull back.

I drove on past him until I reached the fifth house along the private road. The pool was shimmering with reflected sunlight and chemicals as I got out of the car. When I reached the porch, the front door was opened and a leggy-looking blonde gave me a big smile of welcome. She was wearing a red bikini and her small pert breasts had no need of any artificial support. Her hips were narrow and boyish, but her legs were really something.

"Hi, Mr. Holman." She gave me a big friendly smile. "I'm Samantha."

"Hi," I said.

"Please come on in. Mr. Larsen is expecting you."

I followed her inside the house. Her bottom was small and muscular and hardly bounced at all. Larsen was waiting for me in the living room with one elbow propped on the bar. The belly seemed to be sagging a little more over the belt-buckle, and there was a redness to his eyes.

"The noonday gong just rang," he boomed at me. "So name your poison, Holman."

"No, thanks." I looked at the blonde. "Maybe some coffee?"

"Sure," she said warmly. "I'll go make it for you, Mr. Holman."

She went out into the kitchen, carefully closing the

door in back of her. Larsen topped up what I guessed was his martini, from the tall shaker.

"I got your message," he said. "I didn't know what the hell it meant, so I figured you'd explain when you got here."

"I'm not popular with Eddie Braun," I said. "He and Olsen figure the girl had opened her big mouth to me, so they hustled her out of here yesterday while you looked the other way."

He opened his mouth to snarl, then changed his mind. "Who told you that?"

"Julie."

"How is she?"

"Just fine," I said. "On her way back to wherever she originally came from right now."

"I'm glad." He swallowed a mouthful of his martini. "Now, what's this shit about me doing a movie for Stellar?"

"You saw Manny Kruger yesterday."

"He's crazy!" Larsen shook his head disbelievingly. "Gave me a load of crap about doing a remake of the Hunchback, with me playing the old Laughton part. I didn't know if it was some kind of a gag, or if he'd lost his marbles someplace on the way."

"Suppose it was real?" I said.

"You've got to be kidding!" he sneered.

"How old are you, Duane?" I said. "Around forty-five? You're getting too old for the oaters and, anyway, they're pretty thin on the ground right now. A good movie would put you right back on top just now."

"Me, playing the old Laughton part?"

"If you don't figure you could do it..." I shrugged gently.

"Who the hell says I can't do it!" he exploded. "I did a hell of a lot of real acting before I got stuck in this Western groove. I played rep, the New York stage, touring companies! I could do it standing on my ear."

"But not on your *drunken* ear, baby," I said.

I got the bleak stare from the cold blue eyes, while the deep scar on his left cheek whitened with controlled fury. Then he put down his glass onto the bartop very carefully.

"I guess you're right about that," he said.

"Manny is a manic-depressive," I said. "It started out as a lousy gag, but he believed it. He believes anything where the studio's involved. I can make it happen for you, Duane."

The blonde came back into the room carrying a tray.

"Here we are, Mr. Holman," she said brightly. "Please help yourself to cream and sugar."

"Thanks," I said. "Is this part of the training Eddie Braun gives you, or did you learn it all by yourself?"

A startled look came over her face and then she almost ran out of the room. It was like she never existed for Duane Larsen.

"You can make it happen for me, Holman?"

"I can."

"How?"

"You quit drinking, like as of now."

"So I'll have some of your coffee," he said. "And?"

"You confide completely in Manny Kruger. You tell him he's the only one you trust and believe in. The rest of the studio can go fuck themselves, and that does include the guys who made the original approach to you. But you won't tell Manny their names because you figure it would only upset him and bias his fine judgment."

"He'll believe it?" he said incredulously.

"I told you, Manny will believe anything just so long as you massage his manic ego."

"Is that it?"

"No," I said. "There's something else."

"Like what?"

"The truth about Alison Vaile and the tie-in between her and your other friends like Eddie Braun, Charlie Stratton, and Sylvia Maddon."

"I told you the truth before," he muttered.

"I can see it now," I said. "Episode 15 of some lousy television series where everybody's a star. When they run the titles, the big names are only two to a frame. Then, finally, you get a credit which says, 'Also starring.' Then there's a list of maybe eight or nine names, all printed real small, and your name will be at the bottom of the list, buddy-boy. And somebody watching in Cheyenne will say, 'Hey! I remember him. He used to be a big star one time.' Is that what you want, Duane?"

He picked up his glass and had it halfway to his lips before he remembered and put it down again.

"How do I know I can trust you?"

"You don't," I said impatiently.

"I talk with you and then Eddie and his gorilla visit and beat the shit out of me," he said.

"I beat the shit out of Olsen last night," I said. "You don't have to worry about him."

"Also starring," he said, "with my name on the

bottom of the list. I've been on top now for the last ten, twelve years. Jesus! I couldn't take that. All right, Holman, you've got yourself a deal."

"You want some coffee?" I said.

"Fuck the coffee!" He rubbed the back of his hand across his face in a sharp irritable gesture. "Okay. Alison was—is—a goddamned lesbian. She married me to kill the rumors and because she figured being married to a star would help her image and get her work. It didn't. There's something called a marriage contract, right? And she went through with her part, just fine. Used to lie there underneath me like some plank of wood. Enduring it! So I started playing around, drinking too much, and getting the wrong kind of company. Eddie was just fine. He could always provide a girl at the drop of a couple of hundred dollars. He introduced me to Charlie Stratton and I was impressed with that cool English image, and all. And Sylvia Madden. She was richer than rich and a real attractive woman. I figured she found all that big bull star image of mine irresistible. What I didn't know then was she's bi-sexual. She only got into my bed so she could climb into Alison's bed right after."

"And then you got the divorce."

"Right." He nodded quickly. "I didn't mind paying her the seventy-five grand to be rid of her with no lousy publicity. Afterward Eddie told me I was real stupid. I needn't have paid her a dime. Then he proved it. A private showing of a very intimate movie. They'd gotten Alison drunk one night at Sylvia's place. The two of them making long and explicit love together on the couch with Eddie and Charlie Stratton making a long and intimate movie of it at the same time. It wouldn't look good for my image if certain people in the industry saw that movie, Eddie said."

"Blackmail?"

"I needed a lot of girls to keep up my image, Eddie said. His idea was a long-term contract. He'd supply me with girls—a different one each week—so I'd never need to be alone. All this for six hundred bucks a week, cash money. No checks."

"And you went along with it?"

"I figured I didn't have any choice," he said. "But having these goddamned rentagirls around the whole time without any choice, cut off my balls. That's when I started drinking heavily. In a funny kind of a way it seemed better than screwing."

"And after the divorce, with Alison?"

"I don't know. I never saw her again."

"Eddie used the movie to hook you," I said. "For sure, he would have hooked Alison even deeper."

"I guess so." Larsen very carefully didn't look at me.

"Gloria LaVerne?"

"I told you before, I don't know any Gloria LaVerne."

"Charlie Stratton's partner, Lou Ashbury, drowned in his own pool after a big party," I said. "You know anything about that?"

"No," he said. "But if I'd been Charlie's partner I would have been worried about the company he kept. Especially, a guy like Eddie Braun."

"Nothing more?" I prodded. "It's not worth lot, Duane."

"Nothing I can think of right now," he said. "Does

this mean you're reneging on the deal, Holman?"

"No." I shook my head. "A guy called Pete. Early forties, big, and just starting to run to fat. Red hair, and a matching mustache, the tip of his nose a flaming red color. You know him?"

He thought about it for a while. "Pete who?"

"I don't know."

"It's a real vague memory," he said, and thought some more. Then he snapped his fingers. "Got it! When Eddie showed me that stinking movie of Alison and Sylvia, the guy who ran the projector for us looked just like that!"

"It's something," I conceded. "Anything else?"

"That's it." He grinned. "It was hardly the occasion for Eddie to introduce us. As far as I was concerned he was just the hired help."

"Yes," I said.

"Your coffee's cold," he said. "You want some fresh coffee?"

"Why not?"

"Samantha!" His bull-like roar reverberated around the room and the slender blonde came hurrying into the room a couple of seconds later with a bright smile on her face, all eager to please the master.

"Mr. Holman would like some fresh coffee," Larsen said.

"We can forget the coffee," I said. "You ever wonder what your rentagirls do for their boss, Duane? Apart from fulfilling their obvious functions, I mean."

Larsen blinked at me. "I don't get it."

I looked at Samantha and saw the eager smile had

disappeared from her face.

"You know what happened to Julie, honey?" I asked her.

"No."

"She got beaten up real bad," I said, "by Mike Olsen. Because of that, I beat up Olsen real bad last night and he's still in the hospital. I hate beating up on a woman, but I'll do it if I have to, honey. Duane here will even help if you make him mad at you. Right, Duane?"

"I guess so," he muttered. "What the hell is this all about, anyway?"

"My guess is Eddie likes to keep tabs on what's going on," I said. "The people who visit, the phone calls you make. And he's got a built-in informant, right?"

"Why, you miserable bitch!" Larsen swung toward the girl, his face turned a mottled red color.

"Take it easy," I told him, then looked at the girl again. "You see how it is, honey. You don't call your boss and tell him about my visit with Duane here, or I'll be back and we'll take turns in doing something nasty to you."

"I won't call him," she said, in a quavering voice. "Honest!"

"Old Duane here is on the wagon as of now," I said. "So don't figure on sneaking to the phone while he's out cold drunk because it won't happen."

"Goddamned right it won't," Larsen said thickly.

"You sleep with her, you're paying for it," I said. "And, frankly at those prices I don't figure she's worth it. But it's your choice. If you don't sleep with her, tie her to the bed. I mean it."

"From here on out me and Samantha are going to

have a real close relationship," he said. "Shit! It's so obvious when you say it, and I never even thought about it before."

"Nobody's perfect," I said smugly. "And don't forget to call Manny Kruger."

Chapter 8

I had another bachelor lunch in a diner and by the time I was finished it was getting toward mid-afternoon. If I was real smart, I figured all I needed to do right then was make a couple of intuitive deductions and come up with a complete answer that would amaze everybody including myself. Fat chance! I drove home and remembered for what I paid the guy to look after my pool, I should try and get some value out of it by using it sometime. So I had a long leisurely swim, followed by a shower, then got dressed ready for my date, including the .38 in the belt holster. The way Eddie Braun regarded me right now, I planned on wearing a gun to bed.

I made myself a drink and idly wondered how far toward Oregon Julie was, and if she was still standing up in the airplane, with her seat-belt firmly buckled around the tops of her thighs. Being a sex maniac helps with thoughts like that. Then the phone rang.

"Holman," I said, after I lifted the receiver.

"Hey!" a hoarse voice said. "He's still concussed, right? And here was me figuring you for some kind of a masochistic fag."

"Hello, Pete," I said brightly. "Is that lesbian movie you've got the only copy?"

"You definitely have a talent, Holman," he said, "but definitely. It's a shame it's all wasted in this case. As far as I know there's only the one print, and the negative was destroyed." He chuckled. "For services rendered, you might say. But I don't have it."

"You won't mind me saying this, Pete, but I find that hard to believe."

"I don't give a shit what you believe, Holman," he said. "I told you in the beginning there was nothing but grief in this for you. But you had to keep right on stirring. Now, it's your last chance. That is, if Eddie Braun doesn't get you first."

"Eddie Braun scares the hell out of me the way a big fat canary would scare the hell out of me," I said.

"You're talking about just Eddie, and I'd go along with you," he said. "But Eddie has money. That folding stuff hires a lot of help. Professional help, if you know what I mean."

"I could have figured that out for myself," I said patiently. "It's your dime, Pete, so if you've got something to say, why don't you say it?"

"I'm saying the same thing I said before." There was a metallic edge to his voice. "There's nothing but grief for everybody including both Alison Vaile and Gloria LaVerne if you keep on digging. You quit and maybe I can persuade Eddie to forget the whole thing, put it down to experience. He can always get himself a new Mike Olsen. If you don't quit you either wind up with a lot of grief for everybody concerned, or you wind up dead. Or maybe both."

"You talk a lot of shit, Pete," I said conversationally. "I guess you know that, already."

"Eddie's about to put out a contract on you," he said. "Maybe I'll pick it up myself."

"Was it Eddie who put out a contract on Charlie Stratton's partner?" I said. "A guy called Lou Ashbury. You remember him? The guy who was drowned in his own pool."

"You found somebody with a big fat mouth," he said coldly. "It doesn't mean a goddamned thing, Holman, so don't kid yourself. Lou Ashbury is long dead and by now his body will be about moldered away. Nobody is going to prove anything at this stage. Go back to your bull-dyke client and tell her to settle for a peaceful life."

"You're pissing in the wind, Pete," I told him.

"I think I'll call Eddie right now," he said, "and tell him I'm picking up that contract."

I hung up. Swapping threats with a guy who looked like he should be making a living as a circus clown seemed a peculiarly sterile exercise. I made myself a drink and wondered about Pete and his phone call. The problem was, did he really want to frighten me off, or was he trying to make sure I'd keep right on digging by threatening me? It was a good question and I wished I had the answer. I spaced the one drink to last me until a quarter of eight, then went out to the car.

Sylvia Madden answered the door promptly after I had climbed the fifteen steps up to the front porch and rung the doorbell. She was wearing another full-length dress made out of thin silk in a cobalt-blue color. It clung to the ripe curves of her body in all the right places, flattening and rustling whenever she moved. The cap of strawberry-blonde hair was neatly-combed, the large vivid blue eyes were sparkling and there was a welcoming smile on her wide mouth.

"Welcome to the hero," she said. "I heard about it from Charlie Stratton, too. He says Eddie is quite upset."

I stepped into the front hall and she closed the door in back of me, then we went into the living room.

"Making dinner for you is getting to be a habit," she said, as she headed toward the bar. "I hope we don't get interrupted tonight. What are you drinking, Rick?"

"Bourbon on the rocks, thanks," I said.

She made the drinks and pushed mine across the bartop. I picked it up and she lifted her own glass.

"I'm not sure what we should drink to," she said. "A better acquaintance, maybe?"

"I'm for that," I said.

Her tongue licked her lower lip slowly. "Tell me about it, Rick."

"Eddie has a shack up in the hills," I said. "That's where they took me." There was no need to mention Julie, I figured. "The idea was for Olsen to beat the hell out of me as a kind of object lesson. Eddie drove back to town and Olsen was to follow in my car."

"Leaving you all alone and bruised up in the hills?"

"Right. Only it worked in reverse."

"Charlie says Eddie figures on killing you. He's

annoyed—Eddie, I mean—and I guess Charlie isn't too happy, either. Charlie figures violence isn't the answer as far as you're concerned."

"What is?"

She shrugged gracefully. "I don't know if Charlie's figured out the answer as yet. If he has, he hasn't told me."

I owed Duane Larsen something, I thought; not much, but something. And I almost couldn't wait to see him leaping around a cathedral dome as the Hunchback of Notre Dame.

"I just remembered something," I said. "You mind if I use your phone?"

"Help yourself," Sylvia said easily. "There's an extension in my bedroom upstairs if you want to be private."

"It's not private." I walked across to the phone and dialed Larsen's number.

"Duane Larsen," his voice said cautiously, a few seconds later.

"Rick Holman."

"Hey, Rick." His voice was enthusiastic. "I talked with Manny Kruger, the way you said to talk with him. Worked like a charm."

"Great," I said. "How's your friend?"

"Samantha?" He chuckled. "Nervous. Has been since you left. Can't do enough for me. In a funny kind of a way it's giving me my balls back. Right now I can get a hard-on just looking at her."

"You won't want any interruptions," I said. "How do you rate with the private cops at the end of your road?"

"Okay, I guess. I bribe them a little, here and there."

"Bribe them some more right now," I said. "Tell them nobody gets in to see you, and I mean nobody."

"You figure I've got trouble coming?"

"No," I said. "But who knows for sure?"

"I guess you're right," he said. "I don't want Eddie Braun busting in on me again like the last time."

"And maybe taking Samantha away with him," I said. "She's yours, all bought and paid for, right?"

"You're goddamned right about that, Rick," he said. "I'll talk to the guards right away."

"Have a happy night," I said, and hung up.

"All done and done?" Sylvia enquired sweetly.

"Sure," I said. "What's for dinner?"

"Momma's home cooking," she said. "After last night I figured you need something to keep up your strength, or whatever. Clams for starters, then a great big juicy steak covered with onions, and French fries."

"Apple pie to follow?"

"Don't put me on," she said. "Some Irish coffee, and if you're still hungry you can have the rest of my steak."

"It sounds great," I said.

It *was* great. By the time we had finished dinner and were sipping the Irish coffee I felt replete, if not gorged. Sylvia smiled at me across the table.

"What are you going to do now, Rick?"

"Finish my Irish coffee," I said. "It's good."

She pulled a face. "I mean now you've put Olsen into the hospital and got Eddie Braun fighting mad at you."

"Right now I can't wait to make it with you, Sylvia," I said.

"That's nice." She didn't sound that enthusiastic.

"I've never made it with a bi-sexual before," I said. "Not knowingly, anyway."

Her face froze. "What kind of a crack is that?"

"I haven't seen it, only heard about it," I said. "A great intimate movie, they tell me. You and Alison on the couch with the camera in close-up the whole time."

"You're a son of a bitch," she said. "How long have you known about it?"

"I only heard about it today," I said. "You want to slip out of your dress now? I'll rely on you to tell me any little bi-sexual gimmicks I don't know about."

"Is this how you get your kicks, just talking about it?"

"Eddie and Charlie made the movie," I said. "At the time, Alison was still married to Duane Larsen. So Eddie could blackmail Duane because that movie could destroy his big bull reputation around the town and make him look stupid. You can't keep a reputation as the greatest gunslinger on celluloid when people are laughing at you. So Duane's been paying ever since, in money. I wonder how you've been paying, Sylvia, or maybe you didn't give a goddamn?"

"I didn't give a goddamn," she said. "I'm stinking rich and I don't have any reputation to worry about. The night it happened I was drunk out of my mind."

"How about Alison?"

"She'd been smoking and was stoned on dope. I don't think she realized what was happening apart from the fact we were making love, I mean."

"And afterward? How did Eddie use it to blackmail her?"

"I don't know." She avoided my eyes. "When they

showed Duane the film it was the end for him. He wanted a divorce and I guess he paid off Alison to make sure she never talked about it."

"And Charlie Stratton backed Eddie's 'Media-On' and then his partner drowned in his pool," I said. "After a big party where Gloria LaVerne was present. I can't help wondering if she was still present when he drowned."

"Charlie and Eddie made the film together," she said. "There was no way he could use it as blackmail against Charlie."

"I don't figure Eddie ever blackmailed Charlie," I said. "I figure they were partners, and probably still are."

She got up from the table and I followed her into the living room where she walked across to the windows and stood looking out, her back toward me.

"Being a bi-sexual means just that," she said, in a small voice. "I enjoy sex with men, as well as women. I'm not a lesbian, Rick."

"Sure," I said. "I've read the experts."

"I want you."

It was a replay of the previous night. One hand reached up behind her back and unzipped the full-length dress so it collapsed in a soft heap around her ankles. Underneath, she was wearing pale blue silk briefs that clung tight to her hips. The light golden tan still covered the rest of her. She stepped out of the dress and turned around toward me. Her full breasts jiggled gently with the movement, and the large plum-colored nipples began to harden in the coolness of the air-conditioned room. The doorbell didn't ring and that was something to feel greatful for. Her fingertips slid under the waistband of her briefs and, in an abrupt jack-knifing movement, she peeled them off. When she straightened up again I saw below the soft curve of her belly, the wispy V of strawberry-blonde pubic hair that overlaid her slit.

"I don't want to talk any more," she said huskily. "I want to make love. If that sounds a ridiculous phrase to you then, okay, I want to screw."

She walked toward me and didn't stop until her body was pressed up hard against mine. I felt the inevitable reaction as my hard-on stiffened. Sylvia felt it too, and smiled. Her fingers pushed between us and deftly unzipped me. The next moment she was holding my rod in both hands, squeezing it gently.

"Nice," she said throatily. "I want!"

My hands slid around her waist then slowly dropped until they cupped both rounded cheeks of her bottom, first squeezing, then separating them. The weight of her full breasts pressed even harder, flattening against my chest. Her mouth sought mine, fiercely and hungrily, then her teeth sank firmly into my lower lip. My right hand let go of her left cheek, and quickly moved across her flank, until my finger tips brushed against her wispy pubic hair. She spread her legs apart, grunting with satisfaction as my fingers explored the wetness between her parted vaginal lips. Her teeth let go of my lower lip and she pulled her head back.

"Get your clothes off, Holman," she said huskily. "Before I rip them off!"

Who wants to walk around in a ripped suit? I stripped off my clothes fast and by the time I was naked, I saw she was standing there watching me, with both hands cupping her sex, pulling the lips apart so I could see the pearl-whiteness of her hard clitoris. She had been right the second time, I realized, when she said she wanted to screw. Love-making had nothing to do with it. I grabbed hold of her with one arm around her shoulders and the other under her knees, then lifted her off her feet. The couch was big but not big enough, I figured. There was a large lambswool rug on the floor that looked just fine, so I dropped her onto it. And then it began.

A kind of frenzy of kissing and licking and sucking and biting where neither of us was concerned with the other. It was simply a question of self-satisfaction, of building to your own frantic climax and the hell with your partner. Sylvia orgasmed first, screaming out loud and her fists beating my shoulders. Mine came a few seconds later in a series of convulsive thrusts until I finally just lay on top of her completely drained.

"Get off," Sylvia said, in a thick voice, what seemed a long time later. "You're crushing me to death."

My limp rod slithered out of its moist haven and I slowly came up on to my knees. Sylvia looked up at me, a curious look of triumph in her vivid blue eyes.

"I'm sorry about the bi-sexual gimmicks," she said. "I guess there just wasn't time to demonstrate for you."

"The way I feel right now," I said, "you must wear a lot of women out, like completely."

"I can't help it." She raised herself up to a sitting

position then caressed her breasts in an almost loving gesture. "It's just that I always perform better with an audience."

"It was what I'd call a damned good show!" a masculine voice said from in back of me. "None of that simpering finesse you get with a couple of girls. All brute savage lust. Jolly good!"

I looked back over my shoulder and saw Charlie Stratton smiling benignly at me. I also saw the gun in his hand pointing directly at me.

"Yes, it's your gun, old boy," he said. "But there's no reason why you shouldn't get dressed."

Chapter 9

I got dressed. Sylvia got dressed, slipping back into the full-length cobalt-blue dress and zipping it up the back. Then she picked up the pale blue briefs, crumpled them into a soft ball in her hand and tossed them at me.

"A keepsake," she said. "In never-loving memory."

I let them drop to the floor in front of me. Charlie Stratton still had that benign smile on his face and the gun in his hand was still pointing directly at my stomach.

"Call Eddie," he said. "Tell him we have one package ready and waiting to be picked up."

"Sure," Sylvia said, and walked toward the phone.

"I was here before you arrived," Stratton said. "Most of it was very boring, really. You have no idea how banal your conversation was over dinner."

"You mind if I make myself a drink?" I asked him.

"That's very naughty of you, Holman," he said reproachfully. "I mean, we all know what you can do with a near-full bottle. Poor Olsen's still unconscious so I hear. It hasn't improved Eddie's temper at all."

Sylvia came back from the phone. "Eddie will be right over," she said. "Or he'll send somebody to take care of it. He wasn't sure which just now."

"Make your late lover a drink," Stratton said. "What would you like, Holman?"

"Bourbon on the rocks."

"It certainly fits the image."

Sylvia went to the bar and started making the drink. Stratton still watched me carefully as he spoke to her.

"I was enchanted, of course," he said. "I mean, it made up for all that lurking and listening, indeed! But I'm curious, Sylvia, dear. Why all that sudden and violent sex?"

Sylvia smiled at him. "Well, I thought you'd appreciate it, Charlie, and maybe it would make up for a very dull evening. Besides, you know I'm an exhibitionist."

"The movie certainly proved that," he said. "I did so wish I had a movie camera with me tonight. One of your finer moments, my dear."

"It was what he did to Olsen mainly," she said. "All that violence. I wondered what it would be like unleashed. I do mean sexually, of course."

It was like I wasn't there. Sylvia finished making the drink and picked up the glass.

"Give it to him at arm's length," Stratton said. "Just remember where there's life there's hope, Holman. I shall certainly shoot you if you try anything at all."

Sylvia brought the drink across to me and dutifully held it out at arm's length. I took it from her and tasted it. It was a good bourbon on the rocks, and maybe my last.

"I suppose it's known as going out in style, Holman," Stratton said conversationally.

"Gloria LaVerne and Alison Vaile," I said. "The one and the same, right?"

"It seems a very obvious conclusion," he said. "But then you're a very obvious man, Holman. Crude and violent, and no intellect at all, I suspect."

"I don't think I'm going to stay around for the anti-climax," Sylvia announced. "I'm sore in the most intimate places and quite exhausted. I think I'll go take a shower, powder my bruises, then go to bed."

"Whatever you wish, my dear." Stratton beamed at her.

"Good-bye, Holman." She gave me a kind of frigid smile. "The next time I make it with a woman I'll remember you and probably laugh myself sick."

"All it needs is Eddie Braun dead and buried, and everybody else can get back to leading their own lives and pleasing themselves," I said. "Think about it."

"No, thanks." She yawned loudly. "I'm too tired to think about anything right now. See you soon, Charlie. You, Holman, I won't see, not ever again."

As she walked out of the room the thin silk of her dress clung momentarily to the underside of her bottom, revealing all its rounded glory. It was a more poignant farewell than anything she had said.

"Just what did you mean by that exactly, Holman?" Stratton asked, after she had gone.

"What?"

"All it needs is Eddie dead and buried and everybody else can get back to leading their own lives."

"What I said. Eddie was the mastermind, right? You wanted something, Eddie organized it. Duane Larsen wanted to get rid of his lesbian wife and Eddie did it for him. But he made sure it left him in a position to blackmail Duane. A permanent supply of rentagirls, and it didn't matter a goddamn if Duane wanted them or not, he's had to keep on paying six hundred dollars a week for the privilege of having a built-in spy in his own house."

"Duane never was very smart," Stratton said.

"And how smart have you been, Charlie?" I sneered at him. "You wanted to get rid of your partner, Lou Ashbury, and Eddie organized that for you. In return for what? Backing him in 'Media-On.' My guess is that operation loses money the whole time. The only good operation Eddie has going for him is his rentagirl deal. And how big a percentage have you got of that? A big fat zero is my guess."

His mouth tightened. "I have to admit you are correct in your estimates," he said, almost primly. "I have no interest in his rentagirl operation at all. And 'Media-On' is a disaster area. The rent alone for the space they occupy. And the staff he carries!"

"Eddie's been walking tall and carrying a big stick called Olsen," I said. "He doesn't have his big stick since last night. If you want to get out from under, Charlie, now is the time."

"You can't really expect me to trust you, Holman," he said. "Even if you did somehow manage to rid us of Eddie, there's nothing to stop you going to the police afterward and telling them about Ashbury."

"I'm a realist," I said. "There's no way to prove anything about how your long-dead partner died. There's the coroner's decision on record. The only way I could prove anything would be by a signed confession. Is Eddie about to sign a confession? Are you?"

"I take the point," he murmured. "What do you have in mind?"

"You've got your own gun?"

"In my hip pocket."

"Give me back mine and I'll hide it away. You keep your own gun on me when Eddie arrives."

"Supposing he sends somebody else?"

"Then I'll persuade whoever it is to take me to Eddie. With a gun in my hand I'm a real good persuader."

"And suppose you're just joshing me, Holman," he said. "I give you back your gun and you point it straight at me. Then you call the police."

"What the hell would I tell the police?" I snarled. "That I was having sex on the floor with the lady of the house and then I discovered this voyeur was watching us?"

His light blue eyes studied me intently from the gaunt face. "I suppose you're right," he said. "There is nothing you could tell the police that wouldn't sound like wild unfounded suspicion."

"We have to be running out of time, Charlie," I said. "Eddie, or whoever, will be here at any minute."

"You make it all sound very convincing," he said. "I'm trying to remember what your actual interest in all this is?"

"Alison Vaile," I said. "I have to find her, then

remove whatever is stopping her going ahead with some television commercials. Not necessarily in that order, but they are my only interests."

"And have Gloria LaVerne disappear forever?" He grinned at me bleakly. "That could be a lot harder than you think, Holman."

"What the hell is that supposed to mean?"

The doorbell rang.

"We're about out of time, Charlie," I said.

"Yes." He nodded quickly. "The answer to your proposition, Holman, is I don't think so. Tempting, of course, but there's always a question of trust involved in these matters. I'm not sure I could trust you once you had a gun in your hand." He smiled quickly. "But a nice try. I'll grant you that. A very nice try, indeed."

"You'll live to regret it, Charlie," I promised him.

"Which is something you won't do, old chap," he murmured. "Shall we go and answer the door?"

I walked into the front hall with Charlie right behind me with the gun pressed into the small of my back. The doorbell rang again impatiently when we were halfway down the hall.

"Stop for a moment," Charlie said softly.

I stopped and felt the gun withdrawn from my back. "You have to find your client and then remove whatever is preventing her making those commercials," he said. "I can't help you find your client. I don't know where she is. But I do know what's preventing her making those commercials. The film, obviously, Eddie has it, or he knows where it is."

"What difference does it make now?" I grunted.

"I should have thought before," he said. "Don't you have some American phrase about coppering a bet? You can have my gun but I shall keep yours and, while you're here, I'll keep it pointed at you. If, at any moment, I think you're going to renege on our agreement, I shall kill you. Do I make myself perfectly clear?"

"Perfectly," I agreed.

The doorbell started ringing again even more persistently.

"If you leave with Eddie, or whoever is ringing the doorbell, I shall do nothing, of course," he said. "I will sincerely hope you retrieve the film and I shall expect to hear of Eddie's sudden demise in the very near future."

"I understand," I said.

"Good. Here is my gun. A point-three-two caliber. Doesn't compare with your gun, I'm afraid. But then I suspect you are a much more expert shot than me, so I need some advantage. Your point-three-eight caliber would blow a large hole in almost anything reasonably close, I should imagine."

"You imagine right," I told him.

"Here we are then."

The next moment a gun was thrust into my hip pocket.

"It's loaded, in case you were wondering." He snickered softly to himself. "I'm not a sadist, Holman, and I do have high hopes you'll pull this off. Damn that doorbell!"

The persistent ringing was getting to my nerve-ends as well.

"So why don't I open it?" I said.

"Do you think that's wise, old chap? I mean, if Eddie, or whoever, sees you standing there they might react in a very adverse way. Stand to one side and I'll keep your gun pointed at you while I open the door."

I did like he said, then he opened the front door. The guy who stepped quickly inside with a gun in his hand wasn't Eddie, but he was instantly recognizable with the receding red hair and matching mustache.

"Everything is under perfect control," Stratton said quickly.

"So what the hell took you so long in answering the doorbell?" Pete said.

I was just being very careful," Stratton said coldly. "Holman has no gun and, as you can see, I do."

"Okay, so let's get back inside," Pete said.

We went into the living room and I sat down in the nearest armchair. Stratton sat facing me, the gun in his hand still carefully pointing at my stomach.

"I'll help myself to a drink," Pete said, and walked behind the bar.

He set up a glass and then reached for a bottle. "I took Eddie up on that contract, Holman," he said. "I figured you might like to know that."

"Who has the film, Pete?" I asked him.

"What the hell do you care?"

"I figured you did," I said. "How else could you bring Gloria LaVerne back into Alison Vaile's life?"

"You're talking a lot of shit, Holman," Pete said. "Mike Olsen recovered consciousness a couple of hours back but they still don't know if he's got any permanent brain damage."

"He had that before I hit him," I said.

"All that shit you were talking, Holman," Stratton said. "I'm interested."

"Pete here, works for Eddie, right?" I said.

"What's known as a jack of all trades, I believe," Stratton said. "So?"

"So Alison Vaile found herself an agent in Sandy Parker around a year back," I said. "Sandy got her a cameo part in a big Stellar movie then came the offer of the television commercials."

"A sleazy kind of way to make a few thousand dollars," Stratton said.

"Sleazy is a matter of degree, Charlie," I said. "This is a sponsor who wants to go network and make a real big impact. The money he's talking about is a quarter-million dollars."

"I'm impressed," Stratton said.

"And then Pete called her," I went on. "Reminded her of Gloria LaVerne and, I guess, that intimate little home movie. That's where all your troubles started, Charlie. Because Sandy Parker listened on the extension and she didn't like what she heard one little bit. So she hired me."

"It was Eddie's idea," Pete said harshly.

"I've been wondering about that," I said.

Stratton rubbed one side of his face briskly with his free hand. "A fascinating conjecture," he said. "Part of Eddie's master plan, or the hired help venturing into free enterprise?"

"Like I said, Holman talks a lot of shit." Pete glared at Stratton. "Don't be fooled by his double-talk. A couple of minutes to finish my drink and then I'm taking him out of here. He won't ever bother you again, Mr. Stratton."

"There's an easy way to find out," I said to Stratton. "You could always call Eddie and ask him."

"It sounds a very reasonable solution," he said mildly.

"Mr. Stratton," Pete said heavily. "You won't mind me saying this, but you're an amateur. A pro like Holman here, makes his living out of conning people.

Now you and Mrs. Madden corralled Holman real smart. And I'm going to finish the job. Don't make it any more difficult for me."

"I'd like a word with Eddie just the same," Stratton murmured.

"You're being stupid!" Pete said sharply. "I'm trying to be polite, you know that." He picked up his gun from the bartop. "Goddamned amateurs! Now you drop that gun on the floor and listen to me while I talk some sense into you."

"Suppose I don't?" Stratton said coldly.

"One thing I don't want to do, Mr. Stratton, is kill you." There was almost a pleading note in Pete's voice. "Look! Maybe we can figure the whole thing out. There's nothing you need to tell Eddie. I've got a great thing going with Alison Vaile. In the end she's going to make those goddamned commercials and I'm going to get a hundred grand out of her just for keeping my mouth shut about that film. We split fifty-fifty, okay? Think about it, Mr. Stratton. Fifty grand for just being smart!"

"Tempting," Stratton muttered. "Definitely tempting. But you have to think beyond the money, Pete. Eddie will find out. As sure as God made little apples, Eddie will find out. And where will it leave us then, Pete?"

"He don't need to find out," Pete said desperately. "Not ever!"

"Oh, shit!" I said angrily. "I said it myself, right?"

"Shut up!" Pete snarled at me.

"And then you called her," I said. "Reminded her of Gloria LaVerne and that intimate little home movie. And I still didn't get it!"

"Wisdom rarely comes, even to the wise man," Stratton said, and grinned suddenly.

"You're both so goddamned cute it gives me a pain," Pete rasped. "Drop the gun, Stratton, or you're a dead man!"

Stratton took one quick look at him and hastily dropped the gun.

"You're stupid, real stupid!" The tip of Pete's nose looked like it was on fire. "Complicating things like this! Now I got to kill the both of you and figure out some explanation that Eddie's going to buy."

"It'll have to be *some* explanation, buddy-boy," I said.

"It was a reverse situation," he said. "When I got here, you'd taken Stratton's gun away from him and faked the whole situation. I got onto it in time but not in time to save Stratton. You killed him, then I killed you."

I had edged my right hand behind my back during the long, and mostly dull, conversation. Now it hovered above my hip pocket. Now was the time.

"Charlie!" I yelled. "Go for your other gun!"

I would say one thing for Stratton, he sure had fast reactions. He threw himself out of his chair and started rolling frantically across the floor. Two slugs from Pete's gun ripped into the upholstery which would have been protected by Stratton's body a couple of seconds before. And by that time I'd lifted Strattons' .32 out of my hip pocket and pointed it at Pete. He started to swing his gun toward me and the look on his face said he'd only one aim in life and that was to fill me full of holes. I triggered the gun three times in quick succession, because if you figure on killing somebody before they kill you, the smart thing to do is make sure you accomplish your aim.

The first slug took him high in the forehead, the second missed completely, I guessed, and the third slammed into his chest, spinning him half-round so he was facing the far wall. His free hand slammed down onto the bartop, shattering his glass, and then he slowly disappeared in back of the bar. I came out of the chair real fast and checked him out. He was dead. When I straightened up again, Stratton had also regained his feet and was looking at me.

"A right bastard," he said softly. "Somehow, there are no adequate words to describe you, Holman."

"I figured you had fast reflexes, Charlie," I said, and tried not to sound smug.

"And what happens now?"

"Act Two, I guess," I said. "We need a couple more to complete the cast."

"I won't even try to follow your demented reasoning," he said tiredly. "But what about him?"

"Pete?" I looked down at the crumpled body at my feet. "Nobody will see him unless they walk behind the bar. Leave us make sure if anybody makes a drink it's either you or me."

He nodded, then his face suddenly looked even more gaunt. "I just remembered something, Holman. It was my gun you used to kill him."

"A minor detail," I said. "We'll take care of it later. Right now I have to issue an invitation."

I walked out of the room and up the stairs real fast. When I reached the top I stopped and yelled out, "Gloria LaVerne. Come out, come out, wherever you are!" After a couple of seconds I added, "And you've got five minutes at most."

Chapter 10

I cleaned up the broken glass from the bartop, folded Pete's body as neatly as I could in one corner behind the bar, then made fresh drinks for Stratton and myself. He took the glass out of my hand and curtly nodded his thanks.

"I presume you have some kind of a plan," he said, "and, hopefully, it's something that doesn't depend on my fast reflexes again."

"Yes, is the answer to both questions," I told him.

"I don't find that particularly reassuring," he muttered, then gulped down a mouthful of his drink.

I checked my watch and saw five minutes had almost gone already. It took a lot of effort but I managed to stop myself from running up the stairs again. A couple more minutes crept past then I heard one of the stairs creak.

"You are obviously not about to be amazed like

Mrs. Webster of the dictionary fame," Stratton said quietly, "but I do hope you'll be pleasantly surprised."

She came into the living room a few seconds later. A tall brunette, with her jet-black hair spreading out across her shoulders in a kind of controlled abandon. Her hazel-colored eyes looked at me distainfully, then at Stratton.

"I'll have a drink," she said. "Campari-soda."

Thin silk was her fetish, I guessed. She was wearing a harem outfit made from it and semitransparent. The bolero top showed most of her cleavage and didn't quite contain her full breasts, while the pants fit skin-tight to her knees before they flared out and were caught by bangles on her ankles. It was obvious she was wearing nothing at all underneath the outfit.

"A set of different colored wigs and contact lenses," I said. "To quote a friend of mine, Sylvia Madden, how corny can you get?"

"Everybody loved it," she said. "I was a big success at all the parties."

"Especially Lou Ashbury's party, I bet," I said.

She smiled. "He loved every moment of it and got very excited when I said I'd come back after the party was over. You want to know something hysterical, Rick? I was going to push him into the pool the way Eddie wanted, but then he slipped and fell in all by himself."

"She never did have any sense of timing," Stratton almost moaned. "None at all."

"I never heard it, Charlie," I said. "You do just one thing for me, Sylvia—sorry! I mean, Gloria—you call Eddie and tell him everything's just fine. Pete took me away around a quarter-hour back but now you and Charlie are so tensed up and excited with the evening you want to be turned on some more. You want him to bring the film over and run it for the both of you."

"Why should I?" she said coldly.

"Do it," Stratton said crisply. "I've made a deal with Holman. Pete is a corpse behind the bar in case you hadn't guessed. We can come out of this untouched."

"Suppose he won't do it?" she said.

"Right now you're Gloria," I said. "Be Gloria to him. Get petulant if he says no. Say you're bored and if he won't do anything for you, why should you do anything for him. If necessary, say like why shouldn't you call the cops and tell them about the gun and games that have been going on in your house."

"Eddie won't like that," she said.

"But he'll come."

She pouted and was about to shake her head. Stratton stepped forward quickly and hit her across the side of her face. She swayed back with the impact and he hit the other side of her face.

"Do it, dear," he said thickly. "You know how I can be when I lose my temper."

For a moment she just stood there immobile, the imprint of his hand standing out on both sides of her face. Then she shook her head slowly.

"All right, Charlie, dear," she said softly. "I just wanted to be sure, you know?"

"Make the call, dear," he said. "You know nobody can resist Gloria LaVerne when she really wants something."

She gave him a big smile, took a deep breath, and

then started walking toward the phone. The rear view with her bottom bouncing under the tight thin silk was almost enough to get me sexually interested again. But my rod simply didn't want to know. I picked up my drink as she dialed and didn't try to pretend I wasn't listening.

"Eddie?" Her voice was a low sexual caress. "This is your very own Gloria."

She took it from there. After a while I stopped listening and looked at Stratton.

"Whose idea was it?" I asked him quietly. "Gloria LaVerne, I mean."

"Eddie's," he said. "Who else? Eddie has a peculiar gift for looking into people and seeing both their true characters and their fantasies. You take a young, highly-attractive widow like Sylvia. She has more money than she can possibly use, and is attractive enough to get any man she desires. So she's bored. Add the fact that's both bi-sexual and an exhibitionist, and presto!" He snapped his fingers. "Gloria LaVerne was born."

"And Pete was just the hired help who worked for Eddie until he got big ideas of going into the blackmail business all by himself."

"Oh, absolutely," he said.

There was a click as Gloria/Sylvia replaced the phone.

"It wasn't easy," she said. "But he's coming and he's bringing the film with him."

"Well done!" Stratton said heartily. "It's like I told you, dear. The man who could resist Gloria LaVerne's blandishments has yet to be born."

Shades of "Charlie's Aunt," I thought wonderingly. Maybe the both of them were from Brazil because that's where the nuts come from.

Stratton handed her the freshly-made drink and got a gracious smile in return.

"How long will he take?" I asked.

"Not long," she said. "A quarter-hour at the most."

"Just one more question, Holman," Stratton said. "What happens when he does get here?"

"You're going to kill him, Charlie," I said easily.

"I'm—what?"

"Nobody else can," I said. "With Eddie dead there are no more problems, right?"

"And no more Gloria LaVerne," Sylvia said slowly.

"All good things have to come to an end," I said. "This is going to be your last and greatest performance, dear Gloria."

"So I'm going to kill him," Stratton said heavily. "And afterward? I have no wish to seem picky, Holman, but that means we'll have two bodies here."

"You invested in Eddie's 'Media-On' and you've been losing a lot of money, right?"

"Right." He nodded quickly.

"So you wanted to pull out. Eddie said there was something you didn't know about. He ran his rentagirl racket under the cover of the publicity agency and if you tried to pull out he'd involve you in it up to your neck. You thought about it and found it intolerable. So you told him he could do whatever he liked but you were still pulling out. Your friend, Sylvia Madden, invited you over for dinner tonight. Eddie suddenly arrived with one of his henchmen and forced his way into the house. He started threatening you. Threatened your girlfriend, Sylvia. If you didn't go along with him they'd make life hell for you, starting with your girlfriend. They forced you to sit in a chair and watch while they started on Sylvia. Slapping her around, tearing her clothes, abusing her with their hands. You wouldn't stand for it. You went for your gun. As you got up from the chair, Pete took a shot at you. The slug is still buried in the armchair's upholstery to prove it. So you shot him in self-defense. Eddie pulled a gun and shot at you and fortunately missed. So you killed him also in self-defense."

Stratton thought about it for a few seconds. "It sounds all right," he said dubiously.

"With Sylvia to back your story it's cast-iron," I said. "You've got the slug from Pete's gun in the upholstery as proof. When they check out Eddie's background they'll find you're also telling the truth. You *have* lost a lot of money in your investment in the publicity agency, and Eddie *was* running a rentagirl racket."

He took a sudden deep breath and exhaled slowly. "All right. Now tell me the details."

"He rings the doorbell, Sylvia lets him in and brings him in here," I said. "The faster the better, Charlie; just don't shoot him in the back, is all."

"And whose gun do I use?"

"Your own," I said. "And you can give me mine back."

We exchanged guns and I returned the .38 to the belt holster. There was a sullen expression on Sylvia's face, I noted, as she drank her drink.

"Something bothering you?" I asked politely.

"I liked being Gloria LaVerne," she said. "It was fun."

"You can still be Gloria LaVerne," I said, "but for Charlie. A kind of blue-plate special just for him."

"You get Charlie going he's okay," she said. "The trouble with Charlie is he only gets going about once every month."

"It sounds like a problem for Gloria LaVerne," I said. "Like Charlie himself said, the man who can resist Gloria LaVerne's blandishments has yet to be born."

"There's that," she said. There was a brooding look on her face and then it slowly disappeared like she had finally made up her mind. She nodded. "Sure. I don't mind Gloria getting to be exclusive, just so long as she doesn't have to disappear altogether."

The doorbell rang and I guess the three of us jumped.

"What now?" Stratton asked hoarsely.

"Gloria answers the door and brings him in here," I said. "The rest is up to you. But do it fast."

"All right."

There were dark hollows in the gaunt face as he took out the gun and held it ready.

"Play it in character, Gloria," I said quickly.

"Sure." She moistened her lips then gave me a glowing smile. "Eddie will never know what hit him, I promise you."

She walked out of the room in a kind of undulating glide, the cheeks of her bottom under the thin tight silk softly gyrating against each other. She could have made a fortune in the movies, I thought idly, but then she had a fortune already. I moved away from Stratton who stood tensely facing the door with the gun ready in his hand, and stood beside the bar with my own gun ready in my hand. There was the sound of the door opening and then a soft indistinguishable murmur of voices. Then, after too long a time, the sound of the front door closing again. A silence, then Gloria came back into the room with a can of film in her hand.

"He wouldn't stay," she said helplessly. "Just gave me the film and said he had to go."

"He refused Gloria LaVerne?" Stratton said, in a strangled voice.

"I did my best, Charlie," she said. "My very, very, best. I'm real sorry, I—"

I caught a faint flurry of movement in back of her and yelled out, "Charlie!"

Sylvia was pushed sideways and went stumbling across the room. Eddie Braun burst into the room, a gun in his hand, his cold grey eyes burning with fury. Stratton hadn't moved. There was a coldblooded intent about his stance I could have admired at some other time. They seemed to shoot simultaneously. The sound of the shots was deafening as it reverberated around the room. Eddie grew a third eye just above the bridge of his nose and blood began to spurt thinly from it as he fell to the floor. I put my own gun away because I realised I didn't need it anymore. Then I saw that Charlie was also on the floor.

I went over and kneeled down beside him. His right hand was still holding the gun and his left hand clutched his stomach. Arterial blood welled from between his fingers and seeped onto the floor. Then I was roughly pushed aside as Sylvia went down onto her knees beside him.

"I'm sorry, Charlie," she said tearfully. "I really am! But I just couldn't bear the thought of losing Gloria LaVerne. She always had so much more fun than dreary old Sylvia Madden. And I figured Eddie should have an even chance so I told him you were waiting to kill him in here."

"You stupid bitch!" he said. "You finally had to do it."

"Do what, Charlie, dear?"

"Slip right over the edge into paranoia," he said. "I saw it coming but I tried to pretend to myself I was wrong."

"You can still have lots of fun, Charlie," she said eagerly. "When you're better, I mean. You and Gloria will have loads of fun, I promise!"

He made a painful grunting sound, then lifted the gun and fired three shots into her at pointblank range. She slid sideways gently until she finished up on the floor. I took one look then looked away quickly. Her face was an unspeakable gory mess.

"It's better this way," Charlie said. "Maybe five years with a brilliant psychiatrist could have helped her, but there would have been no way to persuade her it was her only chance. And she'd go on ruining more people's lives."

"I'll call a doctor, Charlie," I said.

He shook his head. "Don't bother. I'm dying, Holman, and I have no wish to live in any case. You saw me just commit coldblooded murder. The thought of dying is infinitely preferable to spending the rest of my life in jail." He twisted his head around and looked at me. "There is one favor you can do for me, Holman."

"Name it."

"Please call me Charles. Charlie is so incredibly

vulgar!"

"Sure, Charles," I said.

"Thank you."

He smiled, and the smile stayed on his face as he died. I got back unto my feet and looked around the room helplessly. Then I washed the glasses, dried them carefully and returned them to the rack above the bar. I replaced the bottle where they belonged and figured when the cops were finally called by somebody they could figure out for themselves what the hell had happened, or not, maybe. On my way out I picked up the can of film and tucked it carefully under my arm.

Chapter 11

I pushed the doorbell for the fourth time then held my finger against it. An upstairs light came on and, a few seconds later, the front hall light showed. I took my finger off the doorbell reluctantly and waited. The front door opened a few inches on the chain and a pair of polished blue eyes glared at me.

"Holman," I said. "Let me in."

"At this hour of the night? Or morning, or whatever the hell it is!"

"Let me in," I said, "or I'll beat the door down. I don't really give a goddamn either way."

She hesitated for a moment, then undid the chain and opened the door wider. I stepped into the front hall and she closed the door in back of me.

"Just what the hell is it you want?" she said sharply.

Sandy Parker, as ever, looked immaculate with

not one short straight blonde hair out of place. She was wearing a black belted robe over severely-tailored pajamas, and leather moccasins on her feet. I walked past her and started up the stairs.

"Just where do you think you're going?" she asked tightly.

I didn't bother answering her as I kept on climbing the stairs. She caught up with me just before I reached the top and grabbed hold of my arm.

"Who the hell do you think you are?" she said furiously. "Walking into my house in the middle and the night and acting like you own it, or something!"

I pulled free of her arm and kept on going. A bedside lamp cast a soft glow through an open doorway so I walked straight into the room. The circular outsize bed was rich with a white satin cover and dark wine-red cushions. A blonde head stirred sleepily, then the blue eyes opened and stared at me. There was a sudden gasp of shock and Alison Vaile sat bolt upright in the bed. The cover fell away revealing the plump full breasts and their roseate nipples, and also the vivid scratch marks on the underside of her left breast.

"What's he doing in here?" she said haltingly. "That's that awful man who was in the bar that night and—"

"Don't worry, Miss Vaile," I interrupted her. "I'm just leaving."

"It's all right, darling," Sandy Parker said in a gentle persuasive voice I wouldn't have believed her capable of achieving. "Everything is under control. You go back to sleep."

Alison Vaile sank back onto the bed and pulled the cover up to her neck.

"Don't be long, honeypot," she whispered. "Your little Alison's feeling awful lonely."

"I won't be long, darling," Sandy Parker said quickly. "I just have to say good night to Mr. Holman and then I'll be right back."

I didn't figure I could stomach any more of the pap so I went out of the bedroom and back down the stairs. The living room was easy to find. I switched on the lights and headed toward the bar. By the time I'd made myself a drink, Sandy Parker was in the room. Her face was a mottled crimson color.

"Do you realize what you could have done," she rasped. "Scaring her like that! Alison is a very fragile person and she can't stand any kind of shock."

"Oh, shove it!" I told her.

"What?"

"You conned me," I said. "From the start of it all you conned me, Sandy."

"I don't know what you're talking about."

I took time out to drink some of my drink. It didn't taste like anything remotely recognizable but then my stomach had a problem responding to alcohol, as well. It kept on churning with the frustrated desire for one of my fists to hit Sandy Parker straight between the eyes.

"You knew what it was about from the beginning," I said. "Alison would tell her honeypot anything."

There was a minor satisfaction in seeing her wince when I used the term of endearment.

"Pete worked for Eddie Bruan," I said. "He got the bright idea of blackmailing Alison for money after he heard about the television commercials offer. If she didn't go along with him, he'd show the film to the sponsor, the boss of the network, or whoever. But you didn't trust me, Sandy. So you gave me all that crap about something mysterious must have happened in Alison's life after she was divorced from Duane Larsen. Then the night after I fronted Pete in the bar along with Alison, you told me she'd walked out on you. Another pressure point, right?"

"If you like," she said coldly. "Alison was safe with me. I wouldn't trust anybody else to look after her. Especially you, Holman."

"You gave me the clues, right?" I said. "In a garbled kind of way. Duane Larsen for a start, and then all that crap about Pete calling her Gloria LaVerne on the phone. He never called her Gloria LaVerne, he just mentioned the intimate relationship she'd had one time with Gloria LaVerne, captured forever on celluloid by Eddie Braun and Charlie—Charles—Stratton. Right?"

"They got her so high on marijuana she didn't know what she was doing," Sandy said hotly. "Those depraved people! They deserve—"

"They're dead," I said flatly.

"They're what?"

"Dead," I said. "Eddie Braun and Pete and Gloria LaVerne, alias Sylvia Madden, and Charles Stratton."

"Dead?" Her mouth dropped open. "You killed them?"

"They killed themselves one way or the other," I said. "Maybe it needn't have happened if you'd told me the truth in the beginning. That all you wanted was that film back so nobody could blackmail Alison and she could go ahead and make the commercials."

"If you were as good as they say you are, I figured you'd find out for yourself," she said. "And you did."

"That's right," I said. "I did."

"But you didn't get the film," she said bitterly. "So I'm not going to pay you a dime, Holman. Not one stinking dime! And I'll broadcast it around that you took on an assignment for me and fouled it up completely. Your reputation will be shot full of holes by the end of the week."

I took my time about finishing the drink then said, "I've got the film."

"You have?" Her eyes gleamed suddenly. "That's wonderful! Forget what I just said, please! It was very stupid of me, Rick. Where is it?"

"In the car outside."

"Get it for me," she said eagerly. "Bring it in here so I can burn it. Please!"

"Why the hell would I want to do that?" I gave her one of my nastier smiles. "What was Pete plugging for? Fifty per cent? Sixty? Maybe seventy? I'm not greedy, honeypot. I'll settle for fifty per cent. Let me try and figure that out. What's fifty per cent of a quarter-million dollars?"

"You bastard!" she said desperately. "You wouldn't!"

"Give me one good reason why not?"

"I—" Her mouth open and shut a couple of times but no words came out.

"I can think of a good reason," I said. "You turn me on, Sandy. Lesbians always do. You spend a week with me at my house and I'll settle for fifteen per cent of the quarter-million. How about that?"

The mottled crimson slowly ebbed from her face leaving it a livid white color. Her hands clenched into fists and beat slowly against the tops of her thighs. Finally she made a faint whimpering sound deep in her throat.

"All right!" she muttered.

"You take a week out from your office and from this house, of course," I said. "I'm insatiable where a beautiful blonde like you is concerned, Sandy."

"What about Alison?" The words were wrenched out of her.

"It's only a week," I said. "Maybe she could take up knitting?"

For a moment there, I figured she was about to explode and I would be covered by a fine hail of bits of Sandy Parker.

"Sit down," I said. "Write me a check for my fee. It would be five thousand dollars but I've had a rough ride, so make it seven. I'll go get the film."

She was still staring blankly at the wall in back of the bar when I walked out of the room. It didn't take long to collect the can of film from the front seat of the car and carry it back to the living room. She was making herself a drink in back of the bar and, I noticed, had already made me a fresh drink.

"There's the check." She gestured toward the bartop.

I picked it up and saw it was made out for six thousand, five hundred.

"I said seven," I told her.

"You added two thousand for the rough ride," she said. "I knocked off five hundred for the rough ride you've just given me, Rick. Maybe I deserved it but did you have to be so rough?"

I put the can of film down on the bartop. "I guess a

close relationship is a close relationship, regardless of the sexes of the people involved."

"Is that your profound thought for the week?" She grinned at me icily.

"I guess it is." I picked up the check and put it into my wallet. "It's no use telling you not to do anything I wouldn't do because you can. Right, honeypot?"

Chapter 12

The cleaning woman found all the bodies next morning and it was a big story that day. The day after it was a much smaller story and the police were quite sure nobody else was involved. And the next day some nut who happened to be a marksman, took his rifle up to the top of a water tower and shot five people dead. And that seemed about the end of it.

A couple more days went by and then Manny Kruger called me.

"Hi, there, Rick, old buddy," he said, with immense enthusiasm. "How's every little thing with you?"

"Fine," I said cautiously, "and you?"

"Just great! Everything's coming up roses! We signed the contract with Duane Larsen's agent today and the deal is all set."

"With him playing the old Laughton part?"

"Right! I don't usually make forecasts, Rick, but I have a feeling in my bones that this is going to be a great motion picture. One of the greatest ever made and I have you to thank." His voice was suddenly careful. "Right, Rick?"

"You know me," I said. "Anything for an old buddy."

"That's it?" He sounded genuinely surprised. "I mean, I know I made a bad joke about a percentage interest in the motion picture which would be ridiculous and absolutely out of the question. But a finder's fee? Something?"

"Manny," I said. "When an old buddy can't do something for another old buddy without counting the cost, what are old buddies coming to?"

"Rick!" he said emotionally. "You make me want to cry! But I'll think of something, old buddy. I'll think of something, I promise you!"

I hung up before he started faking snuffling noises on the phone. It got to be late afternoon and I got to feeling bored. The whole evening stretched ahead with nothing more exciting in view than watching television. I had a leisurely swim, put on a toweling robe afterward and convinced myself the evening was advanced enough for me to have my first drink of the day. Just after I had finished making the drink the doorbell rang.

It had to be a mirage, I figured, when I opened the front door. Standing there right on my doorstep was a statuesque redhead who must have been around six feet tall in her high heels. She was wearing a white sweatshirt and black skin tight pants. On the front of the sweatshirt was a vividly-colored transfer of a fighting cockerel and underneath was the caption:

BIONIC COCK. Her full breasts jutted proudly under the sweatshirt and the pants showed off her generously-rounded hips and long legs to definite advantage.

"Hi, there, Rick," Liz Moody said. "I have something for you from Mr. Kruger."

She handed me an envelope, smiled, then walked past me into the house. I ripped open the envelope and there was one of Manny's cards with the single word, "Enjoy!" scribbled across it. In a kind of daze I remembered to close the front door then went back to the living room.

"You *do* have a pool," Liz Moody said. "That's fantastic. I'm going to dive straight into it."

"You know what this card says?" I mumbled.

"Enjoy." Her eyebrows lifted a fraction. "Mr. Kruger was going out of his mind trying to think of something special to give you as a token of his gratitude, so I made an obvious suggestion. You don't like it?"

"Like it?" I said wonderingly. "I love it!"

"So we don't have any problems. That's fixed. But I'm only here until the week-end."

She peeled off the sweatshirt and another bra-less girl was revealed as her full melon-shaped breasts spilled free. Then she kicked off her shoes, unzipped the black skintight pants and carefully wriggled out of them. That left the lemon-colored panties, but not for long. She pulled them off with an expert yank then straightened up. With no high heels she was maybe a couple of inches shorter than me, and all of her was gloriously feminine from the hardening tips of her coral-colored nipples, down past the tawny-red profusion of pubic hair and all the way down her beautiful legs.

"Okay," she said. "Last one in the pool is a scaredy-cat!"

My right hand once again suddenly developed a life of its own. It suddenly made a swift lunge and its fingers grabbed her firmly by her pubic hair.

"That's taking unfair advantage," she said mildly. "Not that I mind too much."

"We can always swim," I said, "like afterward."

"All that energy!" she said admiringly. "I always knew it could be put to a lot better use if I could only get close enough to it!"

THE SPANKING GIRLS   BT51383 $1.50
Carter Brown   Mystery

A beautiful porn star is murdered in the beach house of an eccentric millionaire who is known for his many marriages—always to virgins. Al Wheeler has to find out who the girl really is—and how she got there!

Setting: Southern California, contemporary

DONAVAN'S DELIGHT   BT51382 $1.50
Carter Brown   Mystery

With over 50,000,000 books in print, Carter Brown is one of the worlds most popular writers, and now he joins the Belmont/Tower line with a novel about a man who discovers that the stately manor next door is more sinister than it seems!

Setting: England, contemporary

DEADLY PARTY   BT51374 $1.50
Linda DuBreuil   Mystery

The Governor was a shoo-in for re-election, but it was getting dangerous to support him—his friends were being murdered. Was it a coincidence—or was it part of a more sinister conspiracy? Sloan Malone had to find out before he became the next victim!

Setting: Indiana, 1970's

REUNION   BT51364 $1.50
Richard Russell   Mystery

Davey had been dead a long time, but his teacher still wanted to find out who killed him. She hired Angel Graham—and then the teacher was murdered. The next victim was Gwen Queens, Angel's paramour, and Angel, with Gwen's brother Jeff, had a personal score to settle with the killer.

Setting: New York and New Jersey, contemporary

THE NIGHTMARE MACHINE   BT51372 $1.75
John Nicholas Datesh   Mystery

Suppose you dreamed that you were dying—and you couldn't wake up? Raymond Carleton learned how to control people's dreams. He was a genius, and vengeful. A little sleeping powder made him a murderer. Montgomery had to stop him—but first he had to find out how Carleton did it!

Setting: Pittsburgh, contemporary

GUILTY AS CHARGED   BT51373 $1.75
Elizabeth Hanley   Mystery

All the evidence was circumstantial—no one had found Marge Ratliffe's body, nor could anyone say for certain whether or not she was dead. But her husband Cliff had pleaded guilty to the murder. Even so, some people refused to believe him!

Setting: Illinois, 1930's

DEADLIER THAN THE MALE   BT51160 $1.50
J. C. Conway   Mystery

Four men had been beheaded with no clues, no motive, no suspect remaining. Novice Private Investigator Jana Blake finds her first criminal case a bizarre chain of killings with no real lead. Join Jana as she takes her sleuthing from the subways of Manhattan to its breathtaking conclusion in the sky over the East River! A BT Original.

DOMINIQUE   BT51345 $1.50
R. Chetwynd-Hayes   Mystery

David Ballard didn't like living on his wife's money—he wanted to make it his own. It was easy: he drove her mad, then to suicide. But Dominique didn't stay dead, and Ballard found himself trapped in a maze of hallucinations and hauntings that left him with no way out—except death!

MUSIC TO MURDER BY   BT51262 $1.75
Vernon Hinkle   Mystery

Sergeant Holliman chose his words carefully. "Mr. Webb has established himself in scholarly circles as a superior detective, having the knack for uncovering answers to questions that baffle his colleagues."

"Yes, but in the field of music," suggested Bimbo.

"His solutions are based on a superior intuition," continued Holliman. "In other words, he may be some sort of genius, and I'm ready to take a chance on him."

"Sergeant Holliman," asked Bimbo, "are you asking policemen to cooperate with a civilian rather than the other way around?"

"If you want to put on a uniform again," Holliman said, "cooperate with the librarian, and never breathe a word if he screws up!"

30 MANHATTAN EAST   BT51311 $1.75
Hillary Waugh   Mystery

Detective Frank Sessions worked out of Homicide North. He got the tough cases, and Monica Glazzard's murder was one of them. She was a gossip columnist with a lot of enemies—including her daughter. Sessions' problem was too many suspects!

A GRAVEYARD TO LET   BT51222 $1.50
Carter Dickson   Mystery

Sir Henry Merrivale had solved difficult cases in his long, distinguished career. But this was the most baffling! There was the strange matter of the graveyard—but that was only the beginning... A complicated puzzle by a master of mystery.

THE ANALOG BULLET   BT51220 $1.50
Martin Smith   **Suspense**

Newman ran for Congress, but the experts said he didn't have a chance. No one was more surprised than he was when the computers said he'd won—by a landslide! And computers don't lie—or do they? A political thriller about a young politician who became the victim of a terrifying conspiracy.

Martin Smith is an elegant writer."
—*New York Times*

FINISH ME OFF   BT51324 $1.75
Hillary Waugh   **Mystery**

Another Homicide North mystery! Someone had murdered a hooker, and Detective Frank Sessions had to find the killer before he struck again. But there were a lot of men in her life, and any one of them could have done it!

MINNESOTA STRIP   BT51333 $1.75
Peter McCurtin   **Mystery**

Tracing runaways was the kind of work private eye Pete Shay was used to. It was an easy seven hundred bucks when he took Janssen's money to find the missing Ruthie. He never expected to find himself on a murder case! A new novel from an Edgar Award-winning writer!

CROOKED LETTER   BT51385 $1.75
Linda DuBreuil   **Mystery**

Poison-pen letters were doing their work in Woodsdale, creating an atmosphere of suspicion and hate. Soon the murders began, the sheriff was killed, and the mystery was left to be solved by an alcoholic cripple!
Setting: Midwest, contemporary

SEND TO: **TOWER PUBLICATIONS**
P.O. BOX 270
NORWALK, CONN. 06852

PLEASE SEND ME THE FOLLOWING TITLES:

Quantity	Book Number	Price

IN THE EVENT THAT WE ARE OUT OF STOCK ON ANY OF YOUR SELECTIONS, PLEASE LIST ALTERNATE TITLES BELOW:

Postage/Handling

I enclose...

FOR U.S. ORDERS, add 50c for the first book and 10c for each additional book to cover cost of postage and handling. Buy five or more copies and we will pay for shipping. Sorry, no C.O.D.'s.

FOR ORDERS SENT OUTSIDE THE U.S.A., add $1.00 for the first book and 25c for each additional book. PAY BY foreign draft or money order drawn on a U.S. bank, payable in U.S. ($) dollars.

☐ **PLEASE SEND ME A FREE CATALOG.**

NAME_____
(Please print)

ADDRESS_____

CITY_____ **STATE**_____ **ZIP**_____

Allow Four Weeks for Delivery